8/17

FLYING CORGI

M E D I A

Audrey's Garden

By Leslie Koresky

Flying Corgi Media
Chelmsford, MA

Flying Corgi Media
Chelmsford, MA
www.flyingcorgimedia.com

Text copyright © 2014 by Leslie Koresky
Cover Design © 2014 by Trina Teele
Book Design by David Freedman

Flying Corgi Media and colophon are trademarks of Flying Corgi Media, Inc.

This is a work of fiction. Any similarity to persons or places in existence is purely coincidental.

Cataloguing Data
Koresky, Leslie
        Audrey's Garden / Leslie Koresky —1st ed.
        p. cm.
1. Girls —Juvenile fiction.
2. Bullying —Juvenile fiction.
3. Friendship —Juvenile fiction.
4. Bullies —Juvenile fiction. I. Title

Form/Genre: Juvenile fiction.
ISBN 978-0-9839460-2-1

Printed in the United States of America

ACKNOWLEDGEMENTS

My acknowledgements are heartfelt and many.

I am forever grateful to my son Michael, who told me I was onto something and that I should pull those eleven pages out of the drawer and write until I was done!

Thank you to: Alison Kaelin for her valuable personal perspective; to Elizabeth Williams for her love and support; to all the staff and students at the South Row School for their daily inspiration, and in particular to Principal Irene Hannigan for her constant encouragement. Thank you to Susan Gates and Madeleine Needles who believed in Audrey's story. And my special gratitude to Priscilla Stevens, an editor of intelligence, skill, and a supreme understanding of the human spirit.

Yes, it takes a village.

–Leslie Koresky

Be yourself.

Everyone else is taken.

– Oscar Wilde

CHAPTER

1

The greatest of delights and the best of joys
is to know that people like to be with you,
and to know that you like to be close to them.

– Maxim Gorky

Audrey sat like crumpled paper on the edge of her bed, staring blankly at the wall, face soaked in tears. Who could have sent these hateful notes to her? Ashamed, Audrey was too embarrassed to tell her mother. And with her good friends gone, she was suddenly feeling scared and very much alone. As she absentmindedly rubbed her sore arm, body trembling, she wondered how, in barely a year, her joyful life had become so horrible.

It seemed to Audrey like both a million years ago and just yesterday that her family moved from Boston to Greenwood Springs. Time can be weird that way, she figured. But one thing she knew for sure was how excited and happy she was when her family traded their city apartment for the cute little suburban home she'd always hoped for. And with a yard of her own and trees and grass and everything, maybe even a little flower garden, her life was going to be the best ever in the whole world.

She remembered the day it all began — a moment in time, so chock full of wonderful possibilities.

———————————————

On the day Audrey and her family took a drive with the real estate agent through the small town of Greenwood Springs, she fell in love with its tree-lined, winding streets, cozy houses on patches of green, and flagstone walkways. And she so loved the jack-o-lanterns sitting crookedly on front porches. So different from the city.

The city was where Audrey had lived for the whole ten years of her life so far. Everything was different in the city. It was harder, grayer, and noisier. Her older cousin, Lilabeth, called it a kaleidoscope of whistles tooting, motors whirring, drills riveting, and feet tap-tapping and clip-clopping to necessary destinations. Lilabeth was the "brain" of the family, and could always think up creative writing ideas. She had even won a writing prize and got her picture in the paper. Audrey felt lucky if her own paragraphs had capitals and periods.

Audrey loved downtown Boston. Her mom had begun to take her into town when she was about three or four years old. No trip was complete without a walk through the Public Garden. Sometimes, there would be an elegant ride on the Swan Boats. She loved the way the willow trees drooped their long feathery branches into the edges of the duck pond, and how the ducks would waggle their way across the water, poking their bills into the bits of peanut shells tossed by park visitors. Audrey and her mom would usually get ice cream cones "to go," always mint chocolate chip for Audrey, and never a sugar cone. Mom would lick her cone, and Audrey would bite hers (she liked to look at her tooth tracks in the creamy scoop) while they strolled down Newbury Street, looking at the furs, jewels, and gowns as if waiting for a ball to start, window by heavenly window. Her mom called it an "otherworldly experience." Sometimes, she sounded like Lilabeth.

Boston was great and all, but unless your family had a lot of money, you didn't live anywhere near those brick-lined sidewalks that always wound up on the glossy picture calendars they sold at Christmastime in bookstores. And your windows had no flower boxes or shiny black shutters, either. Basically, you lived in a two-family or triple-decker house with no bushes out front. And if you happened to get a landlord who didn't like kids, you usually weren't allowed to play in the back yard — which was nothing but a patch of cement and weedy dirt anyway.

Audrey lived with her mother, father, and pesty little brother, Matthew, in the second floor apartment of a two-family house on Walker Avenue. She had to admit that it was pretty terrific, really, what with her best friend, Milly, living across the street, their school three blocks away, and the library, the all-time-great place to sit and think, just around the corner.

Once Audrey discovered how much fun it was to lose herself in the depths of an awesome book, the Whitman Library became her most prized destination. She spent so much time there, especially in the summer, that Mrs. Hernandez, the checkout lady, got to learn a lot about her family. She listened to Audrey's stories about Matthew, her five-year old brother, who liked to mess up her cd collection and scramble her dollhouse pieces, or her cousin, Lilabeth, who, at almost fourteen, was smarter than Audrey would ever be in about a trillion light years. Audrey and the rest of her family all called her Beth. Anyway, Beth had just won a freshman writing contest in high school and gotten her short story published in a magazine. A magazine, for heaven's sake!

You might assume that Beth was stuck-up and probably poisonous to be around. After all, Alberta Litwiski, grade five "brain," couldn't get her nose stuck up higher in the air if the back of her head sat on her shoulder blades. Boy, if you didn't get all A's and know the cool kids personally, she would barely give you a good-morning hello — let alone lend you one of her gazillion rainbow pencils, even if you were desperate during a division quiz. Well, not cousin Beth. Lilabeth Katherine Frasier was considered, among her teachers and classmates, to be one of the sweetest and most modest students at Franklin Roosevelt High School, and she was certainly a source of pride to the members her family. Beth never bragged about her grades or accomplishments, and she never made Audrey feel like a silly kid, even though Audrey was a full three and a half years younger. Sometimes, during family visits, Beth would brush Audrey's auburn hair, sending her home with extra hair combs, clips, and colored elastics. It was almost like having an older sister — better, really, when Audrey got to thinking about the harrowing older-sister stories she heard from the girls at school.

Milly, Audrey's best friend, lived across Walker Street and three houses up, toward the Charles Porter Middle School. Walker was a pretty busy city street with a double yellow line down the middle. It wasn't the big main road, but was, as Audrey's mom warned, a major cut-through road. It joined one section of Boston to another, and cars buzzed by frequently and quickly. But Milly and Audrey were "city girls" and knew how to take care of themselves. They jaywalked diagonally across the street when nobody was looking. Milly's mom said "J" stood for "jail," which was where they were going if they kept it up.

Milly Hitchcock had been Audrey's best friend since third grade, when Audrey, new to the class and to the neighborhood, was given the seat next to her. Milly had dark wavy brown hair. She had big dark eyes and dimples when she smiled, which she did frequently.

The October morning that Audrey was introduced to

Mrs. Edison's third grade class at Lincoln Elementary School, she dropped her pink and purple pencil box while attempting to settle herself into her new seat. The mishap forced open the box, spilling the pencils and markers all over the floor. The mess looked like a game of pick up sticks. As Audrey attempted to shrink small enough so no one would notice her, the dark-haired dimpled girl beside her got down and helped her put her things back into their container.

"Thank you," said Audrey nervously.

"Oh, that's O.K.. No problem. My name is Milly," whispered her new classmate. "I like your pencil box. Where'd you get it?"

Audrey glanced surreptitiously at Mrs. Edison and in a small voice hurriedly replied, "I think my mom got it at Bob's School Supply, but I —"

The conversation was stopped short by Mrs. Edison, who interjected, "It's very nice to welcome new classmates, but we need to be sociable at the proper time. Millicent, please take your seat and turn to page thirty-two in your anthology. Thank you. Is everything all cleaned up now, Audrey?"

Audrey nodded her head. Lowering her eyes, she glanced quickly from side to side. Some children were staring at her and giggling, some were working diligently at their desks, and one boy with hair that looked as if it had never been combed was twirling his ruler on his pencil like a helicopter.

In the schoolyard, the two girls had discovered that their

favorite scary movie was *Poltergeist* and that they both loved mint chocolate chip ice cream. They also agreed that grilled cheese sandwiches made the absolute best Saturday lunches. But when they realized that they were neighbors, too, they knew that their friendship was totally meant to be forever. And for the next two years, Audrey and Milly were like two halves of the same whole — like butter and sugar corn, they would say, because you couldn't pull the butter from the sugar. You got the whole thing together, and that's what made it taste so good!

For the past several years, Audrey's mom, Alice, had been working full time as a secretary in a nearby manufacturing plant, saving for the down payment on a house. What with high rents and all, Audrey's dad, Thomas, who worked in computer sales, couldn't do it all alone. That's how her mom explained it. From kindergarten through second grade, Audrey attended the day care program at Carter School, back in her old neighborhood. Since the family's move to Walker Avenue, Audrey had been enrolled at the Elm Street After School Program. But the best news was that Milly was there, too. With your own personal best friend, day care was great. Milly and Audrey helped each other with math and spelling, and brushed each other's hair, and made up jokes about teachers. Mrs. Ansell, the phys. ed. teacher, was named "Anteater" because her face and nose were so long. Ms. Burns, the librarian, was called "Granny" because she had gray hair and liked to bring in homemade desserts; the girls figured she was pretty old, too — maybe forty or forty-five. Milly dubbed their math teacher, Mrs. Crain, "Smiley," because she rarely ever did. Their name game was an extra special part of their friendship, because when a big phony like Alberta Litwiski looked at you as if you were a human hairball, it didn't feel so bad as long as you could whisper a made-up name and your best friend knew exactly what you meant.

CHAPTER

2

One of the most beautiful qualities of true friendship
is to understand and to be understood.

– Seneca

"Audrey, telephone!" shouted Mrs. Tabor from the kitchen.

It was six o'clock on a Thursday evening and Audrey was at her desk trying not to confuse her "ea" words from her "ee" words for Friday's spelling test. If she could finish her spelling homework and do her fractions worksheet quickly, then maybe she could watch some T.V. before bedtime. But then she forgot to figure in the time it took to eat dinner, and worried that it might not work out after all. As she began to daydream about the butterfly-sequined jeans she had seen at the mall, a knock on her bedroom door and the sound of her mother's voice brought her back to her spelling sheet.

"Audrey," repeated her mother, "I said you have a telephone call from Milly. But please don't be on for more than a few minutes; dinner will be ready soon."

Throwing herself down on her purple and yellow quilted bedspread, Audrey reached for the phone on her night table. Neither Milly's nor Audrey's parents allowed their daughters to have cell phones. It was an extra monthly expense neither family could afford. In addition, both sets of parents agreed that their daughters were too young for the responsibility.

"Hi, Mil, what's new besides New England?"

"Audrey, you've been hanging around your dad too long. His jokes are rubbing off on you. Hey, guess what? My mom said you can sleep over tomorrow night. And, not only that! Maybe on Saturday she'll take us to the movies and we can go to the mall and get a pizza or something. That'll be so cool. Maybe your mom will let you get those amazing butterfly jeans! So, do you think your mom will let you? Please, please, please!!"

While Milly was getting back the oxygen she'd lost from speaking without breathing, Audrey hurriedly answered, "Hold on!" and threw the phone on the bed. Standing by her bedroom door, she yelled, "Hey, Mom, can I sleep over at Milly's Friday night? Her mom says it's O.K.!"

Audrey's voice, in the high decibel range, shot down the hallway, landing squarely between her mother's eyes, as she was putting the finishing touches on the evening's whipped potatoes.

Audrey ran into the kitchen. "She's on the phone, Mom — I've gotta get back and let her know. She said her mom can take us to the movies and the mall. It'll be so much fun! I haven't slept over in so long! Please!"

Audrey's mother stood by the stove haphazardly brushing away soggy, stray hairs from the side of her face. A petite woman with large brown eyes and faded auburn hair, Alice Tabor enjoyed her position as family caretaker. Cooking for her family and joining them each night in newsy chatter made her feel happy and thankful.

As Alice scooped the potatoes into the serving bowl and arranged the chicken pieces in the platter, she replied, "You can tell Milly it's fine with me. Now get Matthew, and both of you wash your hands and sit down to eat." Turning to Audrey's dad, who was doing paperwork at the table, she added, "Tom, can you put that work away for a while? Dinner's just about on the table."

With that, Audrey jumped twice, threw out a big, wrap-around-Mom hug, and ran back to her phone to tell Milly the good news.

How many good times had Audrey shared with Milly since the day they'd met in third grade? It would be impossible to count. How many birthday parties and Saturday afternoon movies and Chinese food luncheons — always egg roll, never spare ribs! And how many Friday night sleepovers...

———————————

"I wish," began Milly one cold January evening a year earlier, "that I had my own room and then I would paint a blue sky and white clouds all over my ceiling, and have a big purple bed and a doll house almost as tall as me!"

Pajama-clad, the girls were up on their elbows facing the foot of Audrey's bed. Pillows clutched, feet touching, they were sharing their wishes and dreams.

"I've always wondered," mused Audrey, "what it must be like to have my own yard with swings and a tall slide and stuff to climb. And I could play on them anytime I wanted, all day if I felt like it!"

Milly knew that Audrey was referring to the Tabors' landlord, who never let his tenants use the back yard, which was way too small for a swing set anyway.

"When I grow up," announced Milly, "I'll be a famous writer and very rich and we can live in a big house together with the biggest, best back yard. And a doll house!"

"What about our husbands and children? I'm going to have three — two girls and a boy," replied Audrey. "And," she mused, "we'll live next door to each other and our kids will be friends. We can even have a garden to share, with beautiful flowers in between our yards."

"I'm not getting married," answered Milly quite decidedly.

Audrey drew herself up quickly, legs tucked under, and exclaimed, "You are too! You're going to marry Teddy Arnold!"

Teddy was the little redheaded boy who sat beside Milly that year in fourth grade. He had a crush on her.

Milly just as quickly joined Audrey in the same upright position and answered, "Only if you marry Norman Stevens!"

Blue-eyed and dimpled, Norman was the class heartthrob.

With the mention of both boys, the two friends erupted into uncontrolled laughter, each playfully accusing the other of mad, passionate love. Pillows began to fly until a crashed night table lamp brought Mrs. Tabor to the door — officially ending the evening's commotion. But never the fun…

After a second call to dinner, Audrey ran to drag Matthew from under his bed, where he was looking for his LEGO pieces that the family always seemed to be stepping on and kicking around. So many little colored pieces wound up under chairs and appliances that it was amazing that Matthew had any left at all. Brother and sister haphazardly washed their hands and found their seats at the kitchen table. Dad was setting the table while Mom was filling the last empty glass with water. As Matthew began to drink his water, it seemed to Audrey the perfect opportunity to cross her eyes and pull down the corners of her mouth at Matthew. When he giggled suddenly, water shot out of his nose and dribbled down his chin, making a wet spot on his T-shirt and a small puddle on his plate.

The water show caught their father's eye as he took his seat.

"Matthew, can't you behave yourself for two minutes?" cried his dad in exasperation.

"Its not my fault! Audrey made me do it. Tell Daddy, Audrey! You made a face!"

Both Audrey and Matthew sat still, expecting their mom's wrath to come down on them. Dad could get annoyed, but Mom could really punish you if you misbehaved. And she especially didn't like any trouble at the dinner table. Audrey began to get afraid that now her mom might not let her sleep over at Milly's. Why did she have to make that stupid face?

Audrey held her breath and waited for the reprimand and whatever horrible other thing might follow. But, as her mom brought the last of the platters and her dad said how delicious everything was, Audrey had the feeling that luck was miraculously on her side this evening. Mom didn't so much as glance her way, and instead appeared to be gazing at her father in a preoccupied manner. Audrey let her breath out slowly, wondering if she should speak or wait for someone else to begin the dinner conversation. Never one to stay silent for any length of time, Audrey opened her mouth to talk about her invitation. However, before so much as a sound could escape her throat, her father addressed her and her brother.

"Your mom and I," he announced, "made an appointment with Mr. Hartnet to look at a house tonight in Greenwood Springs. That's why I came home earlier than usual and why we're eating earlier than we normally do. We're all going together, because this is an important family decision and we want your opinion — especially yours, Audrey."

Audrey started to get happy butterflies in her stomach. Maybe she'd finally have a home of her own with her own yard, just like kids had on T.V. shows and in the movies. With an upstairs and a downstairs, and pretty bushes in the front and a place to put a jack-o-lantern for Halloween. Sometimes she'd walk by Margie Kramer's house on Sullivan Street and wonder what it must be like to have a house like hers, a whole private house where you didn't have to share a hallway with other noisy families. Then she began to get too afraid to believe it might happen. What about that blue house with the white shutters that she loved and they didn't get, or the one with the huge girl's bedroom that she imagined could be hers — but never would be? Now she didn't think she could finish her chicken and spinach. She was too excited.

Audrey turned to Matthew and said, "Hey, Mattie, won't it be too cool to have a back yard to play in?"

Matthew looked up from his plate, smiled enchantingly, and returned swiftly to resume road work on his Mount Mashed Potato Highway.

It had become increasingly evident at mealtime that Audrey's five-year-old brother had a future in city planning. Hardly a dinner would go by without an elaborate display of roads, mountain paths and parkways. Matthew had a few favorite foods, but was especially fond of mashed potatoes for their pliability. Tonight's plan was particularly awe-inspiring, with its complicated arrangement of overpasses, tunnels and mountain chains. Well-placed pieces of chicken served as rush hour traffic, and the lush roadside greenery appeared courtesy of Matthew's chopped spinach.

Audrey watched Matthew with a disgusted sneer. Boy, Mom and Dad had to be thinking of something else not to notice the sickening mess he was making. This would definitely rate no dessert…

"Now, Audrey," warned her mother, "please don't get your heart set on something. You never know how these things go. I don't want you to be too disappointed, like you were at that last house we looked at. It has to be the right house at a price we can afford. O.K.?"

Audrey nodded.

"O.K. then!" her mother said. "Let's finish up, and Dad and I will do the dishes when we get home."

Audrey had just remembered that she had never gotten a chance to do her math worksheet, but decided to say nothing. Maybe she could tell Miss Hughes tomorrow that a family emergency came up and she wasn't able to do it. Yeah, that sounded pretty good, she thought.

After the dishes were put into the sink and the table and counters were cleaned, everyone got ready to leave.

"Audrey, the ride to Greenwood Springs takes almost half an hour — time enough for you to complete your math in the car. And if you have any trouble, I can help you with it."

Audrey wondered how her mother knew about her math. Boy, it was tough getting away with anything around here, she thought, as she slipped into her blue parka.

One by one, the Tabors left the apartment. Her dad locked the front door in their second floor hallway, and Audrey couldn't help but wonder if this might be the night of her dreams.

CHAPTER

3

If we build on a sure foundation in friendship,
we must love our friends for their sakes
rather than for our own.
– *Charlotte Brontë*

Miss Hughes was collecting the last of the spelling tests. Most of the children were engrossed in their independent-reading books, except for George Philips and Alec Highley, who were trading jokes and making faces at the girls. Audrey was midway into a story about a haunted mansion that had been highly recommended by Milly, who was now beginning a story about a classroom mystery. The girls always assisted each other in selecting reading material. It was so much more fun than studying library booklists, even though Miss Hughes was constantly encouraging them to do so.

Usually, if Audrey really loved the book she was reading (like this one), she would lose track of the world around her until one of her classmates had to whisper that it was time for recess, or art, or lunch. But today, she was finding herself re-reading paragraphs two or three times, looking up from her book to stare out the window onto the parking lot, or just being wiggly and itchy all over. Audrey was ready to jump right out of her skin from excitement. She had to tell Milly, but decided to wait till after dismissal, since this was the day she'd be sleeping over at her house, and she wanted to save it for when they would be alone together.

Last night the house guy (she had forgotten his name) had showed her family a really nice house. She wished that there had still been enough daylight so that she could have seen the outside of the house a little better. What she was able to see seemed very pretty. But the best, best part was the inside. It had a front hall and a real dining room and bedrooms on the second floor. It had two bathrooms instead of the one they all shared now. The bedroom that would be hers was even painted yellow and would match her quilt. And the house had a T.V. room in the basement — all painted and carpeted.

"Oh, Mattie! Look at the stairs!" cried Audrey, as she took his hand and followed the adults to the second floor.

It was a small house, smaller than the last two they had looked at, but sweet, with a good-sized master bedroom and two small rooms for the children. The present family had recently painted the daughter's room yellow and white and the son's blue and white, a detail that did not go unnoticed by Alice Tabor.

"You know, Tom," noted Alice, "we can just move the

kids' things right in without any redecorating, and the rest of the house is in fine condition."

When Audrey heard the comment, she began to get excited. Maybe this was the one. She hoped more than anything that it would work out this time. Please, please, she thought, as she crossed all the fingers on both hands, don't let it be too expensive, like that blue one.

As Mr. and Mrs. Tabor talked in the master bedroom Mattie ran around the blue and white bedroom in a big circle, arms stretched wide and making motor sounds.

"Hey, Audrey!" shouted Mattie, "Look, I'm an airplane!"

As Audrey approached the bedroom door, her little brother was in full airliner mode, swooping, dipping and finally crash landing onto the floor.

"Look how high we are! I'm in the trees," he cried gleefully, now leaning on the windowpane.

The branches of a large oak tree were close to the window. It was not a sight he was used to on Walker Avenue.

"Cut it out, Mattie," whispered Audrey. But she couldn't really be angry when she felt so happy and excited. "Come see my room! It's so big and it's yellow!"

Matthew gladly followed his sister into the next room where he proceeded to rev up his motor for a second flight.

After looking at the house for some time, the family followed Mr. Hartnet (that was his name) back to his office, where they did a lot of talking about numbers and complicated things that Audrey didn't understand. It was now eight-fifteen, and Matthew was getting worn out and obnoxious. The realtor had given him crayons and paper, but he was too tired and cranky, and he threw them on the floor. Audrey found a kid's magazine and began looking at pictures of baby gorillas in Africa. But after a while, she just wanted to go home. Before long, however, her parents were shaking hands with Mr. Hartnet and gathering assorted coats and gloves for the trip home.

As soon as they started down the road, Matthew cried and then fell into a peaceful sleep. It was now almost nine o'clock, but Audrey was too excited to be tired.

"Are we going to buy the house?" Audrey was crossing her fingers on both hands.

Her mother turned in her seat to answer. "Well, Daddy and I made an offer on the house, but now we have to wait and see if the owners will accept it or not. That means that if they like the price that we are able to pay, we can buy the house."

"When will we know?" asked Audrey, whose heart was now beating like the drums in the July Fourth parade.

"We just need to wait until the owner calls back and lets Mr. Hartnet know. Then he will call us."

She knew she wasn't supposed to, but Audrey was imagining how her bed, bureau, and pink chair would look in the room, and if her curtains would fit, or if she would get new ones. She was picturing birthday parties in the back yard and holiday meals in the dining room, and, her favorite, a jack-o-lantern on the front steps. And then she got scared that none of this would ever happen. But after a while, as brick and steel buildings whizzed by and cars and trucks whooshed down the white broken-lined highway, Audrey's thoughts became muddled in a black-white, black-white, black-white trance, until she fell into a gentle slumber.

───────────────

And then, on Friday morning as the Tabors were busy passing one another in the narrow hall accompanied by assorted hairbrushes and bath towels, the phone rang. Unaccustomed to hearing the shrill sound at seven forty-five in the morning, everyone froze (except for Matthew, who at that moment, was deeply entranced by his eighteen-inch fire truck and ladder). Audrey and her mom were transformed into department store mannequins as Tom Tabor listened intently to the person on the other end of the line — the person that might, might, might be Mr. Hartnet…

It was a scene that Audrey had dreamed so many times in both her sleeping and her waking life that she came to believe it would always remain a dream. As Audrey's dad hung up the kitchen phone, he slowly turned to Alice with a dazed expression, and announced, "We are now officially the proud parents of a 30-year mortgage! I think I have to sit down!"

Audrey didn't know what her father meant, but she knew one thing — that she couldn't sit anywhere. She couldn't stand anywhere. She couldn't seem to be anywhere for longer than thirty seconds. She was beside herself with joy. That yellow painted palace of a bedroom was hers. That yard, that staircase, that Home of Their Own!

Audrey left the house, nearly missing the bus, wearing one blue sock and one orange, and carrying only part of her math homework — having dropped a page on her bedroom floor.

Her distraction continued through the morning, when she mixed up her numerators with her denominators, then into the afternoon, when she found, to her disgust, that she had accidentally ordered salad instead of chicken fingers for lunch. And now, at two forty-five, as she read the first page of chapter three of her independent-reading book for the fourth time, she still couldn't figure out what was going on.

At three o'clock, the class got their coats and backpacks and waited for the bus announcements. Milly waved to Audrey from across the room with her usual dimpled smile. Together they were to wait for Mrs. Hitchcock, Milly's mom, in the front office. As they walked down the hall together, arm in arm, Audrey thought she would burst before she could tell her best friend the amazing news.

CHAPTER

4

The language of friendship is not words, but meanings.
It is an intelligence above language.

– Henry David Thoreau

"Oh, Aud, you should have seen Alberta's face when Michelle got a higher grade on the reading test. She was, like, so angry and surprised! It's too bad you weren't sitting closer."

Milly and Audrey were sitting at the Hitchcock's kitchen table biting into fruit-flavored Popsicles.

A very long thirty seconds passed, and then Audrey spoke. "I have something incredible to tell you, Mil."

Milly was about to speak, when Audrey blurted out, "We're buying a house! Our own house! And you can hang out and sleep over and everything!"

"Oh my God! You are so lucky! You mean, like, no more mean landlords and noisy people downstairs?" asked Milly.

"Nope! And it's got an upstairs with bedrooms, and mine is painted yellow and white, and we'll have two bathrooms and a yard! And, a dining room just like my cousin Beth's house. There's even room for a computer desk, so we don't have to use the kitchen table. Isn't it so exciting, Mil?" Audrey just about ran out of breath.

Milly had put her raspberry Popsicle on her plate.

"So what neighborhood is it in?" she asked.

There were some neighborhoods in town, Elm Park, for instance, where Lilabeth and Uncle Frank and Aunt Bette lived, that were quiet and pretty. As far as Milly was concerned, a house on a street like that would be a joyous relief from the cramped second floor apartment she shared with her parents and three-year-old sister, Sara. Home at 327 Walker Avenue was a shared bedroom, a single overused bathroom, and a living room you could barely get the whole family into at one time, let alone a guest or two. And the upstairs neighbors fought a lot.

"It's not in Boston at all. Remember those houses I told you about last week? It's out there — in Greenwood Springs! I bet stupid Alberta will be speechless when she finds out!"

At that moment, Audrey's heart beat fast with the excitement of a secret finally shared. And at that same moment, Milly's heart broke with the realization that her best friend in the whole world would soon be leaving.

After a silence that hung as heavy as wet laundry, Milly said softly to her best friend, "But Audrey, that means you'll be moving far away."

Audrey enthusiastically replied, "Oh, Mil, Greenwood Springs isn't that far. It only took my dad a half hour to get there. It's really not far at all."

"You'll be in a whole different school. We won't be able to see each other every day like we do now. No more day care together. No more "Secret Name Game." No more studying together. I bet we won't even be able to do sleepovers much anymore. And anyway, you'll be going to school with other kids and you won't have any time for me anymore."

Audrey was so happy, and Milly wanted to be happy for her, and she was. But she was sad for herself. Suddenly, tonight's rented movie and popcorn and tomorrow's trip to the mall seemed sad to Milly. Everything seemed sad. She wanted to cry but kept it inside.

Audrey slurped the last morsel of frozen fruit from the stick, and lunged at her friend with a big bear hug.

"No, Milly, never! We're best friends for life, no matter where we live. I promise I'll call you all the time, and we can still go to the mall, if our moms will take us! After we move in, I'll ask my mom if you can sleep over for the weekend. And I'll come back here to visit a lot. After all," she joked, "who will keep me up to date about Alberta and Michelle? I'll probably have some stories to tell you about my new school, too."

At the thought of Audrey in a new school, the lump in Milly's throat set off a large tear that traveled slowly down her right cheek. Licking the salty liquid from the downturned corner of her mouth, Milly made the selfless decision to be happy for Audrey and to try to enjoy the fun weekend they had planned.

Just then, Milly's mom put down her newspaper on the living room sofa and walked into the kitchen carrying little Sara. She hadn't been able to help hearing a lot of the heartfelt conversation, and felt badly for the girls, especially for Milly, who was already feeling left behind.

As she removed a few crackers from a box to give to Sara, Milly's mother began energetically, "How would you like me to make your favorite for dinner tonight?"

Milly shouted, "Hot dogs on toasted rolls with beans in brown sugar?"

This was followed by the simultaneous shriek from both girls, "And chocolate pudding and whipped cream for dessert?"

At that, Milly, Audrey, and Mrs. Hitchcock began to laugh. If the girls weren't finishing each other's sentences they were speaking identical words.

"Dinner will be ready at about six o'clock. Milly, Daddy is working late tonight, so he won't be eating with us. Why don't you girls go play until dinner time? I'll keep Sara here with me so she doesn't bother you. And after we eat we'll have popcorn and watch a movie. O.K.?"

Audrey and Milly happily set off to riffle through Milly's cd collection, forgetting for the time being the changes they would soon be facing.

      After they ran down the hall to Milly's room, Mrs. Hitchcock removed what remained of their Popsicle sticks — one licked clean, and the other abandoned in a large pink puddle.

CHAPTER
5

Friends are not only together when they are side by side,
even one who is far away is still in our thoughts.

– Ludwig van Beethoven

The holidays seemed to come and go swiftly. The Tabors
had planned to have Thanksgiving dinner this year at their
place, as they usually alternated years with Beth's family.
But because they were dismantling their apartment for the
upcoming move, they spent the holiday with the Frasiers for
the second year in a row. The arrangement was perfectly fine
with Audrey, who loved spending time at Beth's house.

As Christmas approached, the Tabors' apartment
took on the appearance of a warehouse — bare floors with
rolled-up rugs and packing boxes of various sizes and shapes.
Bookshelves were on their way to being empty, and rectangular
discolorations hung on walls where family pictures used to be.
Since a tree was out of the question and all of her mom's holiday
doodads were packed deep in some box, Audrey decided that

it was beginning to look a lot like Christmas everywhere but at the Tabors'.

It was a bleak, cold Saturday, the first day of school vacation, and three days before Christmas. Audrey and her mom had just returned from the mall, where Audrey had purchased a gift for Milly with some of her saved allowance money. Quickly removing her coat, hat, and gloves, Audrey set to wrapping the special present that she'd bought her friend. Gold paper, silver ribbon, and a big shiny red metallic bow. Perfect!

"Can I go over to Milly's today?" Audrey asked her mother, as she gave her little treasure one more round of inspection.

She couldn't wait to give Milly her gift, wondering what Milly had for her. The girls had been exchanging Christmas and birthday gifts since they met. The first year of their friendship, they gave each other the same exact Disney movie! That's when their parents started teasing them about being so much alike. For Audrey's recent tenth birthday, Milly bought her the Harry Potter book she wanted. Milly's tenth birthday was not until April, so Audrey had plenty of time to think of something totally awesome.

Putting some items away, Mrs. Tabor replied, "Well, call Milly first and see if it's all right with her mom."

Before Mrs. Tabor finished her reply, Audrey was racing

down the hall to her room. After a brief phone conversation, Audrey returned to the kitchen, gift still in hand, breathlessly informing her mother that not only could she come over, but that she could sleep over as well (which was a particular treat, considering the sad and sorry state of her empty, box-filled room).

"Are you sure you don't want to go over after dinner? When Daddy and Matt get out of the movies they'll be bringing home some pizza."

"No, that's O.K. Milly said they're going to order Chinese food! I'm going to have egg roll!"

"Well, honey, I think that beats out pizza! Don't forget your change of clothing and pajamas and bathrobe and slippers. And take your toothbrush, too."

Audrey interrupted her mother's list of reminders. "Mom, I'm ten years old, and I've done this a million, trillion times!"

As Mrs. Tabor smiled, Audrey ran back into her room to collect clothing, hairbrush and her latest mystery novel and the girls' favorite cds. Forgetting her toothbrush, she stuffed the lot into an oversized backpack. She grabbed the gold-wrapped present and, dragging the bulging nylon bag into the kitchen, found her coat, hat, and gloves, which she had hastily thrown over one of the kitchen chairs.

Audrey remembered to be careful crossing Walker Avenue. A busy city street at three forty-five on a dismal day could make for a dangerous situation if you weren't watching where you were going. As she made her way to the other side, Audrey saw up ahead the lighted living room windows of Milly's second-floor apartment, and she couldn't wait to get there.

"Merry Christmas, Audrey," sang Mrs. Hitchcock as she put down Audrey's bag and helped her out of her coat. Audrey removed her hat, uncovering a mop of tangled, fly-away auburn hair that sat slightly above her shoulders.

"Milly has been calling you for most of the afternoon. Were you and your mom doing some last-minute shopping?"

Audrey got close to Milly's mom and said in a quiet, conspiratorial voice, "I got a Christmas present for Milly. It's really special, but don't say anything. I want to surprise her."

Smiling, Mrs. Hitchcock answered just as quietly, "Well, Audrey, don't let Milly know I told you, but she's got something for you, too. Honey, why don't you take your bag down the hall to Milly's room? She's waiting for you."

As Mrs. Hitchcock turned to help Milly's little sister Sara with her fingerpainting project at the kitchen table, a small, dark-haired form bounded suddenly down the hall, startling both her and Audrey.

"Hi!" yelled Milly. "What took you so long, Aud? Did you bring your cds?"

With that, both girls made for Milly's bedroom door, Audrey carrying her backpack of goodies and holding the gift behind her back. She carefully laid the gift down, hiding it with her bag, and the girls threw themselves on Milly's bed.

Milly shared her room with Sara. It was decorated in pink and purple. She and Sara had matching comforters in pink flowers on a purple background. The curtains were plain pink with ruffles and the floor was covered in a brick-patterned vinyl tile, because the wood floor underneath was in bad condition, and the landlord wouldn't repair it. Milly's mom promised she would buy a nice rug for the front of the beds soon. Milly didn't really mind. What really bothered her was having to share a room with her sloppy little sister, whose silly baby toys were always everywhere — sometimes even strewn across Milly's own bed. Also, they each had their own teddy bear collection, but Sara insisted on playing with Milly's.

"Look at this dumb baby mess!" complained Milly. "I can't believe I have to look at these plastic blocks and stuff. You're so lucky that you don't have to share your room!"

"Yeah, but Mattie gets into my stuff anyway. Last week he pulled all the books out of my bookcase. Mom says I should be more patient, because he doesn't rip them and he just wants to read. Oh, brother!" she added, as she rolled her eyes in mock frustration.

It was a friendly ongoing game of "Let's Compare Problems," and it gave the girls great comfort in the knowledge that one friend could always sympathize with the other. As in the Name Game, they were in it together.

Milly moved closer to Audrey and, with a slight twinkle in her eye, said, "Michelle called me today. You'll never guess why!"

Audrey's eyes were wide open, as in anticipation of an exciting drama ready to unfold. She knew that Michelle didn't normally call Milly, and she couldn't imagine what caused this strange turn of events.

Before Audrey could utter a guess, Milly answered. "Well, remember that story I told about when Michelle got a better grade than Alberta, and Alberta told her she probably couldn't keep it up?"

Audrey nodded her head in deep interest as Milly filled her in on the latest classroom gossip.

"Well, so then Michelle said to Alberta that she wasn't the boss of everybody. She got real popular after that! Oh, and remember Harriet Reid? Well, she told Taylor Mahoney that Bobby Ketchum likes her and now she turns red every time she sees him."

Milly went on with several more tidbits about the kids in Porter Middle School. Audrey responded with gasps, giggles, and roars of laughter, as well as several stories of her own that put Milly into fits of hilarity as well. After the last belly laugh and final piece of gossip, Milly and Audrey turned to each other at the same moment and blurted out in unison, "So what did you get me?"

After falling upon each other and then back on the bed

in spasms of laughter, each girl got up to find her gift.

Milly opened her gift first. She carefully pulled away the shiny ribbon and bow, tearing away at the smooth, gold paper. Inside the package was a white music box piano that played, "When You Wish Upon a Star." Milly gasped with joy. Audrey knew it was her favorite song.

After a big thank-you and an affectionate embrace, Audrey opened her gift. The thin rectangular box was wrapped in green and red Santa paper and tied up in a white bow. With paper and ribbon tossed aside, Audrey removed from the box what appeared to be a picture and frame. Upon closer inspection, she saw that it was a poem written across a faint pastel picture of two girls on a bench. Audrey read the poem:

> No matter where our lives may roam
> Just down the street, or far from home
>
> Sailing on the open sea
> Tending hearth and family
>
> The bonds we've made will never sever
> For you and I are friends forever.

"Friends forever," Milly said.

"Forever," repeated Audrey, "and ever."

CHAPTER

6

…the joy of it all, when we count it all up,

is found in the making of friends.

– Anonymous

Standing in the doorway of Mrs. Antonelli's fifth grade classroom with her new principal, Mrs. Delahunt, Audrey was struck by how much bigger and busier it was than Miss Hughes' room back in Boston. Actually, when Audrey thought about it, all of Blossom Hill School seemed pretty much brighter than Porter School back home. A light blue vinyl tile covered the floor, and the extra large windows seemed to spread sunlight into every corner. Mrs. Antonelli was the math and science teacher, so posters displaying math rules and procedures adorned the white painted walls. Science mobiles hung from plant hooks installed near the windows, and colorful science picture books were on display along a table against the back wall. The Book Corner offered a great variety of books on animal and plant life. Even the desks took some getting used to. Back at Porter, her desk had a front opening through which she had to carefully slide in and out her papers and books. Her new desk had a slightly slanted top that opened on a hinge, leaving a flat, stationary strip of wood with a carved pencil tray. Today and for the whole first week or so, Audrey would keep leaning over to remove books, only to remember that the top needed opening. One of the first things she noticed as a new student was that most of the children had bottles of water sitting on their desks, alongside pencils, little pencil sharpeners, and erasers. This was amazing to her, because at Porter School no one was allowed to have bottles of water at their desks, and students could only get a drink during recess, lunch, or nurse and bathroom visits.

Mrs. Delahunt gently urged Audrey forward. She walked slowly and unsurely toward her new homeroom teacher, who was writing on the board. Boys and girls were busy with various chores. Some were sharpening pencils, and others were congregated at a bulletin board doing some job that Audrey couldn't figure out. Assorted groups were chatting and fooling around. Three boys were talking hockey scores, and a bunch of girls in a close huddle were tittering at something. A boy with dark spiky looking hair and freckles across his nose had thrown some small object halfway across the room that was nearly caught by a short redheaded boy wearing an oversized football T-shirt. Some students were quietly working at their desks or reading, and some looked up and watched Audrey as she made her way to Mrs. Antonelli.

Turning slightly from her work, Mrs. Antonelli noticed Audrey beside her, and exclaimed, "Good morning. Are you our new student?"

Audrey was so overwhelmed by the newness of her surroundings that she forgot how to speak and simply nodded her head in a "yes" motion.

"And your name? I'm sorry, dear, but I'm a little disorganized this morning and I forgot."

"This is Audrey Tabor," Mrs. Delahunt put in, "who comes to us from Boston." By this time, all the students had caught sight of their principal and were quiet — and turning to stare at Audrey.

With that, Mrs. Antonelli smiled broadly and put out her right hand, replying, "Of course — Audrey! Well, Audrey, welcome to our class and to our school. I hope it will be a wonderful year for you. And don't worry about feeling strange. You'll get used to the routine after a while. I'm going to place you with a very helpful group of students."

As they shook hands, Audrey glanced quickly around the room and noticed that desks were arranged in clusters; again, it was different from back home in Boston. The principal turned to leave, and Audrey whispered, "Thank you, Mrs. Delahunt."

Mrs. Antonelli led Audrey to an arrangement of desks located by the windows. Shortly after being seated, Mrs.

Antonelli asked the students to finish their morning chores and find their seats. It was only after she had taken her new seat that Audrey noticed how young and pretty her new teacher was. She had dark brown hair worn in a ponytail and large dark eyes. She wore a long brown fringed skirt and a light blue sweater, on which was pinned a plastic rainbow with the words, "Science is Life!"

Mrs. Antonelli took this settling-down time to introduce Audrey to the class, suggesting that in the coming days they might show her around and help her feel welcome. Everyone stared again. Audrey felt like a freak.

Later, as Audrey followed the students while they lined up for computer class, a tall chubby girl with long, curly, sandy-colored hair and a beautiful smile walked along with Audrey and introduced herself.

"Hi, I'm Gretchen Hart!" she said to Audrey.

Audrey was so excited to have somebody talk to her that she almost gave Gretchen a hug!

Gretchen continued before Audrey could reply, "Did you really move here from Boston?"

"Uh huh. We just moved to Greenwood Springs at New Year's."

"Oh, wow, Boston!" answered Gretchen, enthusiastically. "Did you get to go to the Aquarium and Science Museum and stuff? Sometimes my mom and dad take me and my brothers there. Was Boston fun? I've lived here since I was a baby."

Gretchen reminded Audrey of Milly; the same energy and animated conversation! She thought about how Milly had helped her pick up her pencils on her first day at Porter School in the third grade. It kind of made her feel happy and sad at the same time.

As they took their places in line, Audrey began to describe her life in Boston, her family, and her new situation. They apparently lived four blocks away from each other, and Gretchen had a seven- and a twelve-year-old brother. She thought Audrey's five-year-old brother sounded cute, and Audrey wrinkled her nose in disgust at the suggestion, explaining how Matthew got into her things, played with his food and drove her crazy. Gretchen offered horror stories about the tyranny of an older brother who "thinks he's a real big shot when he really isn't." The girls continued talking as they approached the computer room. They made sure that they took adjacent seats, although conversation was quickly replaced by computer work.

After computer class and into the next hour and a half, Audrey and the class labored through writing assignments with Mr. Howard, and then went back to Mrs. Antonelli for fractions, which proved to be confusing to Audrey. She was a little behind the class, and thankful that being new had spared her from being called on to give answers. Mrs. Antonelli assured her that she would catch up, and promised that she would work with her, if necessary.

At twelve thirty, Gretchen and Audrey ate their homemade lunches together in the large noisy cafeteria, and before recess, exchanged telephone numbers. Although no one in her class beside Gretchen seemed especially friendly toward her, Audrey figured that it would just take time, as Mrs. Antonelli had assured her.

The afternoon wore on with social studies and reading, and by the time school let out, Audrey was overwhelmed and exhausted. She was looking forward to coming home to her new beautiful room in her new beautiful house in her beautiful new neighborhood. A great school, a brand new home, and a nice friend. Greenwood Springs was feeling like the perfect place.

CHAPTER

7

No man ever got very high by pulling other people down.

– Alfred, Lord Tennyson

Audrey and Gretchen continued to enjoy each other's company, discovering many similar interests and tastes — chocolate ice cream cones (Audrey's second favorite after mint chocolate chip), the colors pink and yellow, scary movies, and hot dogs. Over the first few weekends of their friendship, they watched movies at Gretchen's house and had dinner at Audrey's. Audrey couldn't help but think how much Milly would like her new friend and how much fun it would be to introduce them and maybe hang out all together some Saturday.

"I love your room!" said Gretchen, as she studied the little boxes, perfumes, and hairclips on Audrey's bureau. "Pink and yellow are two of my favorite colors," she added as she sat on the puffy flowered bed quilt.

Audrey was really proud of her room. Her mom had

put up new ruffled yellow curtains and bought a soft pink rug which sat at the foot of her bed. The new rocking chair with its yellow pad made everything just perfect.

Gretchen spied a book lying open, face down on Audrey's night stand. Picking up the mystery novel she exclaimed, "I love this writer! Have you read her other stories?"

Audrey answered, "I've read the one about the haunted schoolhouse."

"With the creepy teacher who dresses in black?" added Gretchen, eyes wide as saucers.

Audrey's heart skipped, so happy to know that she and her new friend even liked the same scary books.

Gretchen went on, "There are about six or seven haunted mystery books in the series. I've read a few. I can loan some to you if you like."

With that, Audrey crossed the room to her bookcase. She pulled out four hard cover books of similar size and design. "Well, if you like mysteries, these are awesome!"

For the next ten minutes the girls sat side by side on the floor flipping through books and exchanging favorite scary stories, until Gretchen got up to take another look around her friend's room.

Glancing at Audrey's desk, which was covered in school books and worksheets, Gretchen stopped abruptly. "Hey, this is neat! Where'd you get it?"

In Gretchen's hand was the framed friendship poem that

43

Milly had given Audrey for Christmas. Audrey had it sitting prominently on her desk, so that she could glance at it from time to time while doing her homework. She was just as proud of Milly's gift as she was of her new room.

Audrey told Gretchen about Milly, about how they met, the things they liked to do, and how much she missed being with her. In the few weeks that Audrey and Gretchen had hung out together, Audrey had noticed that Gretchen appeared not to have any best friends of her own. It seemed weird. Gretchen had lived in Greenwood Springs almost her whole life. She was nice and a lot of fun. You'd think that she'd have at least one really great friend. Maybe she had a friend that moved away, too. Audrey decided to ask her.

"So, do you have any friends you've known for a while?"

Gretchen became still. The bright, animated face suddenly became dark and serious. She looked away, as if she might cry. Audrey was very sorry and embarrassed that she had asked what looked to be a very painful question. She was just about to apologize and change the subject when Gretchen sank into the rocking chair and slowly answered.

"Hillary Wright was my best friend since preschool. She lives a few streets away from me. We used to do everything together. We'd do sleepovers and go to the movies and in the summer I'd swim in their pool and have cookouts. Then her father and Jessica Morton's father got friendly and started golfing together, or something. Now they're all one big happy family. They don't even use their pool so much anymore, since the Mortons take them to their fancy country club all the time. My mom says, 'Good riddance,' but that's easy for her to say."

Pulling her desk chair out and sitting, Audrey interrupted: "Is she one of the kids in our class? I can't remember everyone's name."

"No," answered Gretchen. "She's in Mrs. Richardson's homeroom class down the hall. But Lindsay Brentoff — you know, the girl who sits by the front board; she's got the long blonde ponytail and those fancy hairclips. Well, the three of us — Hillary, Lindsay, and I — were best friends for a while, but she and Hillary don't speak to me anymore. They hang around with Jessica Morton now." Gretchen's face looked both angry and sad.

Audrey waited for the story to continue, but when her friend stopped speaking, Audrey said, "I don't understand. How can you have best friends who just don't want to be friends anymore? Did you have a fight? Did you make them mad? Sometimes Milly and I would get angry with each other, but we wouldn't care about it by the next day." As a second thought, Audrey added, "Who's Jessica Morton?"

It was becoming clear to Gretchen that Audrey had no experience with girls like these, and needed to have a lot explained to her. She almost didn't know where to begin.

"Jessica Morton is in Mrs. Richardson's class with Hillary. Jessica just about rules the fifth grade. She's got long, thick brown hair, the coolest clothes — whatever is new, she's wearing it. She one of the smartest kids in school, and her parents have a lot of money. She makes fun of people, and everyone wants to get on her good side. But the teachers love her because she's so smart and really polite to them. Basically, she can get away with anything around here."

"But," asked Audrey, leaning forward in her chair, "why did Hillary and Lindsay stop talking to you?"

Gretchen shifted in her chair, as if trying to find a comfortable spot. Twisting the ends of her curly hair and then pulling at her T-shirt, she answered in a very small voice, "They started telling me I should lose weight, and that I wore dumb clothes, and that if I went on a diet maybe I could look better. So I tried to eat, you know, lots of healthy stuff and fewer desserts. But it was hard, and I guess I gave up. When we would get together, I started noticing that they weren't including me in their conversations, and they wouldn't call me back when I left messages. And then, finally, I would see them downtown together on Saturdays. They just stopped calling. But the worst of it is that when I walk by them in the hall or cafeteria — if they're with Jessica — they all whisper and laugh. I know they're talking about me, but if I say something, they'll just call me a sensitive baby. I just want to hit them. I haven't told my mom everything. She just thinks that we're not hanging out anymore. I wouldn't want her to call their mothers or anything. I would just about die."

Gretchen looked down at her sneakers and then up again at Audrey. With great hesitation she asked, "Do you think I'm fat, Audrey?"

With the most grown-up sounding reassuring voice she could muster, Audrey answered, "I think you're perfect, Gretch, with the best curly hair and blue eyes of anyone!"

Gretchen smiled warmly and shrugged.

Audrey never heard of anything so mean. What made these girls think that they were queens of the school? She knew that Alberta back at Porter School was really snobby and unfriendly, but Audrey had never noticed her being this mean — even if she did think that she was the smartest person on the planet. Audrey was suddenly glad that she had become friends with Gretchen. Maybe she could help her forget about these other girls. And maybe she could have Milly come and visit. She knew they could all be good friends together.

Audrey knew that she needed to say something kind right away, before Gretchen began to cry.

"I'm so sorry, Gretchen. I didn't mean to upset you. I can't believe how mean they are. I'm glad you told me, though, because now you and I can just ignore them. And I want you to meet my friend, Milly. I know you guys will like each other. We can hang out some Saturday — maybe next week if her mom will let her."

"I'm happy you moved to Greenwood Springs," said Gretchen, "and I'm glad we got to be friends. And if Milly is as nice as you are, then I can't wait to meet her!"

Just then they were startled by a knock on the bedroom door.

"Girls," called her mother on the other side of door, "how would you like us to order a pizza for dinner?"

Audrey promptly opened the door, and both girls answered with a resounding "Yes!"

Pizza, an "On Demand" movie, and a friend on a Saturday night. What could be better? Milly. Maybe next week.

CHAPTER

8

The better part of one's life consists of his friendships.

– Abraham Lincoln

By midwinter, Audrey was discovering that the downside of home ownership was longer working and commuting hours for both her parents and less time at home for herself. Both Matthew and Audrey's day began with a 7:00 a.m. drop-off at their respective school day care programs, although Audrey was quick to point out that her program was called "Kids Club." But regardless of the moniker, it was followed by six hours of class followed by more day care in the school cafeteria. Snowy weather slowed the time even more, as it took parents longer to commute to and from their work.

However, to Audrey's delight, she was joined by Gretchen in the afternoon program. Throughout January, the girls would quiz each other on spelling words and give mutual aid in math. They shared markers, poster paints and cheese crackers.

Audrey began to notice that Gretchen had a lot more drawing ability than anyone she had ever known. But when she would compliment her pictures, Gretchen would usually shrug and change the subject.

"Want to hear some jokes?" asked Gretchen suddenly, as she fished through her backpack.

Audrey was skeptical, but as Gretchen read from a well-worn soft cover joke book, Audrey began to giggle in spite of herself. Soon the girls were bent over laughing at some of the dumbest jokes either of them had ever heard.

It was always fun until four thirty or five in the afternoon, when Audrey would watch with disappointment as Gretchen would leave with her mom. From then on, the day dragged. By the time Mrs. Tabor would arrive at about six o'clock, the room had pretty much thinned out, leaving a quiet straggle of tired children burned out on arts and crafts projects, some with their heads down on tables, others absent-mindedly flipping through picture books.

Over the course of the next few weeks and into the February vacation, Gretchen's mother realized that the relationship between her daughter and this new little girl was developing into a lovely friendship. Mrs. Hart was more grateful than anyone could ever know for the presence of Audrey in her daughter's life.

Since the inexplicable disappearance of Gretchen's best friends, she had become worried at the way Gretchen was keeping quietly to herself. Her child's eyes, once exuberant and bright, had gone dull, and her little mouth seemed always to be turned down at the corners. Irene Hart had tried desperately to make up for the loss that her daughter had suffered by taking her out for Saturday lunches, movies and shopping trips. These diversions made Gretchen happy, but Mrs. Hart knew that they didn't satisfy her daughter in a truly long-lasting way. When it came right down to it, there was no substitute for a real friend. And so, when Gretchen asked if both Audrey and Matthew could come home with her every day and wait for their mom at the Harts' house instead of spending time at daycare, Mrs. Hart couldn't think of a better arrangement — and neither could Mrs. Tabor.

Everyone was delighted. Mrs. Tabor didn't have to feel rushed and guilty as she sat in traffic trying to get to the school. Mrs. Hart watched her child, who had been like a wilted flower, come back to blossom. Audrey was happy to spend extra time with her new-found friend, and relieved that she didn't have to wait endlessly anymore to leave day care, and Gretchen was smiling again, because she had found a nice friend.

As winter played itself out, Audrey and Gretchen did what girlfriends do — listened to music, watched movies and ate pizza, read magazines, complained about their families, and made jokes. Often, when Gretchen's older brother, Eric, wasn't taking over the driveway with friends, the girls spent time shooting baskets. Their amazing lack of skill sometimes sent them into spasms of laughter. Audrey and Gretchen were steadily developing the language of friendship. And with Mrs. Hart's baked treats and unlimited access to the Hart brothers' old truck collection, Mattie was in after-school heaven.

Sometimes in conversation, Audrey would mention to Gretchen something that Milly used to say or things she and Milly used to do together. Gretchen became increasingly curious about this "best friend," and asked many questions about her, wondering why they hadn't had a chance to meet.

————————————————

Since moving to Greenwood Springs in January, Audrey and Milly had called each other several times, talking a great deal but, somehow, never being able to secure a visiting date.

Finally, in mid-March, Audrey got her chance when Milly came for a weekend sleepover. The plan was for Milly to spend Friday evening and all day Saturday alone with Audrey so that they could have time to catch up. Then, on Sunday, Audrey, Milly, and Gretchen would spend the day together.

The greatly anticipated Friday arrived at last. Audrey made it miraculously through a whole school day without major catastrophe, although she could hardly remember anything she learned. And now it was 5:04 p.m., two minutes after the last time Audrey checked the clock. Milly was scheduled to arrive at about five, and Audrey's mom had gotten out of work early for Milly's first visit.

Audrey was too excited to concentrate on anything for

more than thirty seconds. She read the first sentence of her mystery book and couldn't remember what she had read. She put on the T.V. and shut it off. She ran upstairs to make sure her room was perfect. Everything was in place. Her clothes were hung up and her desk was cleaned. She had finally removed her worn sweater, pants and socks from her rocking chair, placing them in the hamper, and had thrown her stack of disheveled papers into her top desk drawer. She knew Milly would be crazy about everything — her room, her house, her neighborhood, everything. She couldn't believe how excited she was to see Milly. Just as Audrey watched her digital clock turn to 5:10, the doorbell rang. Bolting to the bedroom door, she heard loud voices all talking at the same time. And as she made her way down the stairs, she saw her mom hugging Milly and Mrs. Hitchcock.

"Wow," said Milly, looking around, "this is amazing!"

At that moment, Milly looked up to see Audrey bounding down the stairs toward her.

"I can't believe you're actually here!" exclaimed Audrey.

With that, the girls embraced with delighted screams. While Mrs. Tabor and Mrs. Hitchcock conversed in the living room, Audrey took Milly on a very talkative house tour. Although cozy and lovely, the house was modest by middle-class suburban standards — certainly by Greenwood Springs standards — where many homes were large, elaborate and impressively landscaped. Even so, it was jaw-droppingly gorgeous for cramped apartment dwellers like Milly and her family. With three bedrooms and another bathroom on the second floor, a dining room, a fireplace in the living room, and a great family room in the basement, Milly decided that her friend must be rich. And while she was so happy for Audrey (because Milly was always happy for her friend), she felt a little envious of all that she seemed to have.

Once they got to talking, however, it was like they had never left each other. Milly and Audrey fell easily into their old patterns of conversation. But now catching up was in order, and questions needed to be answered. Sharing Audrey's quilted bedcover, like old times, the girls brought each other up to date. Milly began.

"Alec Highley won the fifth grade spelling bee, and Alberta came in second, and she's really mad, too! She thought she was going to win, like she did last year. No one was expecting Alec to do so well, but he's a lot smarter than people think. I think he could be one of the smartest kids in school if he stopped hanging around with his jerky friends who fool around all the time."

It so happened that those very insightful observations were strongly shared by both Miss Hughes and the school principal.

Milly continued with the latest developments on the Boston home front. "Hey, guess what! Michelle and I have been hanging out together most of the time. She isn't friendly with Jennifer anymore and hates Alberta. She's really very nice when you get to know her. You'd really like her, Aud. It's too bad we all didn't get friendly before."

Audrey felt suddenly sad, but didn't know why. She was glad that Milly had a friend since her move to Greenwood Springs. But she felt like she had been quickly replaced and it made her angry. But she knew she had no right to be angry; after all, Audrey herself had found a new friend. She certainly couldn't expect Milly to have no friends now that Audrey was someplace else.

"Well, actually," replied Audrey, "I've got a new friend, too. Her name is Gretchen, and I've been wanting us all to get together. I've been talking about you so much that she can't wait to meet you. I thought maybe Sunday we could do something."

"Oh, hey, that would be great. I can't wait. What's she like?" asked Milly.

Milly felt oddly replaced by not just another girl but by another house, another town, another school, another whole world. She was having scary feelings that she was losing something big. She didn't know why she was having these feelings, and she tried to tell herself that she was mistaken.

Audrey went on to describe Gretchen, what she looked like, her personality, her preferences. In many ways, Milly and Gretchen were quite similar.

Soon the girls gladly left behind the surprisingly

painful subject of new friends, turning their attention to the all-important matter of the weekend agenda. On Saturday, Audrey would show Milly around town, point out her school, neighborhood playground, the town green, Wilson's Apple Orchard, and the old covered bridge. Maybe they'd get an ice cream at Davis's Dairy Farm — something that they never had in the city. Maybe pizza and a dvd for Saturday night. She knew it would be fun. She hoped that Sunday would be fun, too.

Audrey had been nervous about Milly and Gretchen liking each other, but soon after their introduction on Sunday morning, she realized that she had nothing to be nervous about. The three girls talked amiably over a pancake and bacon breakfast in the Tabor kitchen, joined by Mr. and Mrs. Tabor and Matthew. Mrs. Tabor asked a few questions about school, teachers, and what was going on in the old neighborhood. Mr. Tabor glanced at the business section of the Sunday paper, looking up occasionally to tease the girls and make them giggle. When Matthew began to blow straw bubbles into his milk and construct pancake trenches, breakfast was officially over for him. Soon the table, and the day, belonged to Audrey, Gretchen, and Milly.

After a tour of more downtown landmarks, a trip to the mall, Chinese appetizers for lunch — courtesy of Audrey's mom — and a visit at Gretchen's house, Milly said goodbye to Audrey's new friend. For the rest of the day, until Mrs.

Hitchcock's arrival, Milly and Audrey talked.

Running her fingertips across the framed picture she had given to Audrey, Milly said softly, "Will you forget me, Aud? Everything's so great here. And you and Gretchen have such a good time together. Will we really be best friends always?"

Audrey quickly embraced her friend and replied, "Are you kidding, Mil? We'll see each other a billion zillion times!"

Twenty minutes later, Mrs. Hitchcock was saying goodbye to Audrey's mom in the front hall and the girls were hugging each other one last time before Milly and her mother made their way back to Walker Avenue.

CHAPTER

9

He's my friend that speaks well of me behind my back.

– *Thomas Fuller*

Mid-March turned to mid-April, and it seemed that both Audrey and the forsythia were budding and about to bloom. She was getting good grades in her studies and developing an easy familiarity with her classmates. Greenwood Springs was "home" now, and so there was no "back home" anymore — except when she visited Aunt Bette, Uncle Frank, and Lilabeth.

"Hey, Audrey! I think you've grown since the last time I saw you!" exclaimed Beth, as the Tabors entered the Frasiers' living room.

"And your hair is so long," observed Audrey. "It's gorgeous!"

Beth, at fourteen, was clearly taking on the enviable combination of "beauty and brains."

As the girls walked toward the kitchen and family room,

Audrey inhaled the delicious perfume of Aunt Bette's Easter dinner — cured ham dripping with maple, and turkey browning and crackling in its basted juices. How many wonderful meals had she eaten at the Frasiers' dining room table, she thought? How many times had she and Beth laughed at some private kid joke, trying not to choke or spit out the food they were holding precariously in their cheeks? Did anyone howl so uncontrollably at his own jokes as Uncle Frank? (Mom always said his laugh was the funniest part of the joke.) And Aunt Bette just smiled patiently at all the antics surrounding her — an oasis in a sea of craziness.

Matthew knew a good thing when he saw it, and was already on Uncle Frank's lap eating a peanut butter cup when the girls entered the family room. Audrey figured that Mattie's chocolate mustache — before dinner — was not going to make Uncle Frank real popular with her mom.

As Audrey was thinking about Matthew's predicament, she was suddenly grabbed around the waist and kissed on the head.

"How's my favorite niece these days?"

Aunt Bette, smelling like Sunday dinner, turned Audrey around and planted a big favorite-aunt style kiss on Audrey's cheek. Audrey responded, as always, with a bear hug around her aunt's waist and a kiss in return.

"Tell me all about school and your new place," said Aunt Bette, basting her glistening turkey.

For the next ten minutes Audrey proceeded to describe her teacher, her friend Gretchen, the most amazing bedroom ever in the world a girl could have, and how nice it is to live in a quiet suburb. As she took another breath to continue, Lilabeth grabbed her hand and whisked her away.

"Well, 'bye, I guess, Aunt Bette!" laughed Audrey, as she followed her cousin up to her room.

Snuggled under the eaves, Beth's refuge was a powder blue and white dream, furnished with an old blue padded rocking chair, a bureau, and a dressing table with a matching bench (an heirloom from the girls' grandmother). Her white-painted bed was adorned with a blue and white flowered quilt, and a vintage baby blue Princess phone sat atop its base on the matching nightstand. But the centerpiece of the room was the enormous bookcase whose shelves flanked both sides of the little shuttered window. Beth's growing library had been a long-standing source of great joy for Audrey. Books were borrowed and pored over, then returned and replaced by still others. Dr. Seuss to E. B. White to J. K. Rowling. And who knew what yet undiscovered stories awaited? Beth always trusted Audrey with her prized collection.

Beth stood in the middle of her room, pursing her lips at her cousin, who was just about to pull a book down from the shelf. Beth decided that Audrey needed her hair to be French braided — immediately. As Audrey sat happily at Beth's dressing table, Beth brushed and braided and talked about the boy who had just asked her to her first Spring Dance at school. Whispering and giggling, the girls exchanged stories about classmates, and talked of school intrigues. Audrey told Beth about Gretchen and the awful girls.

"...and they don't even talk to her anymore, Beth. It's so mean because Gretch is maybe the nicest person ever." Audrey spoke as she played with the pearl handle of her cousin's silver hairbrush. "If she hadn't told me," she continued, "I never would have known that Hillary and Lindsay even knew her, let alone were her friends!"

Lilabeth leaned in closely to her younger cousin, placing her hands gently upon her shoulders. "Audrey, there are lots of girls like that. They're mean and you have to stay away from them."

Audrey thought for a moment and asked, "Do you know anybody like that at your school?"

"They're at my school, your school, everywhere. They're probably at college, too. I just hang out with my own friends and try not to get too close, you know? We have Dana and Roberta. They never have anything nice to say about any of the other girls. They even talk about each other. They probably gossip about me, too. They can if they want to. I don't care."

Beth was as serious as Audrey had ever seen her.

"Yeah," answered Audrey, "but you don't have anything to worry about. You're perfect!"

"I'm not perfect, Aud. Nobody is and nobody needs

to be. But I'm O.K. And so are you and so is Gretchen. We don't need the mean girls."

The girl talk continued for the next fifteen minutes until they were called to dinner.

It was a wonderful afternoon, as usual. Uncle Frank got rid of the peanut butter cup evidence. Mattie didn't spill one thing (except he couldn't resist making an impressive mountain underpass out of his whipped sweet potatoes). Alice Tabor laughed at Uncle Frank's joke — way before the punchline. Tom Tabor made three puns, at which only Alice laughed. Beth gave Audrey a new set of hair clips, and Aunt Bette smiled brightly as everyone told her what a delicious, fantastic dinner she'd prepared. Especially, for Audrey, the yummy chocolate chip cake.

As a yellow-drenched afternoon turned gradually to purple-grey, the Tabors hugged the Frasiers and headed back to Greenwood Springs. Home.

CHAPTER

10

You can hardly make a friend in a year,
but you can lose one in an hour.

– *Chinese Proverb*

April had brought daffodils and green grass. It also brought a case of spring flu to Gretchen. Poor Gretchen was in agony with a throat like razor blades, a body full of aches, and fever chills. (Yuck!) Audrey promised to bring the class homework to her — for when she started feeling a little better. Mrs. Hart arranged to pick the work up before dinner every night.

Although Audrey lost her cafeteria companion, she wasn't wanting for company. She fell into easy conversation with Keisha and Micah from her class group. Almost four months at Blossom Hill made her more accepted by just about everyone. Of course, her mom always said, there are some people who just aren't friendly, and there's nothing anyone can do about that.

On Tuesday, the second day of Gretchen's absence,

Audrey was finishing her school lunch and preparing for recess when she felt someone quietly approach. Looking up slowly, she saw a tall, slender girl, blonde hair pulled back severely into a high ponytail, short denim skirt and bright pink sweater that could be missed only if you had your back to her.

"Hi!" said a soft, pleasant voice.

After a three or four second delay, Audrey realized that the ponytail and the voice belonged to Lindsay Brentoff. Audrey quickly looked around to find the recipient of this greeting, but could find no one. Most of the children at her table had left to get their coats for recess. The only stragglers, beside herself, were Arnold Peters and Douglas Baers, who always looked as if they were just pulled out of a dirt pile. Lindsay couldn't have been speaking to them.

Lindsay continued, "I couldn't help but notice your hair today. I love French braids. I think they're so cool. And yours looks great. Do you do them yourself?"

Audrey had been in Miss Antonelli's class since the beginning of January, and in all this time could not recall Lindsay Brentoff ever speaking a single syllable to her. This was weird.

With slight hesitation, Audrey replied, "Um…Thanks. Actually, my cousin taught me how to do them, but my mom helped me with this one."

"Well, if you can manage all this hair," Lindsay said, as she grabbed and tossed her long ponytail, "then maybe you can teach me sometime. Are you going to finish those chips? I'm still starving. I only had yogurt today."

"Oh," answered Audrey, a bit off balance by the sudden request, "sure, you can have them. I'm done."

Audrey watched in fascination as the prettiest girl in class daintily ate her chips with with fingers tipped with perfectly polished nails, while her pink and silver star earrings dangled against her neck. Audrey suddenly felt clumsy and oafish. Getting up from the table, she readjusted her jeans and sweater, which now seemed baggy and altogether out of style. She was hoping that she could manage to not trip over her sneakers or bump into a trash can on her way out of the cafeteria.

Just as Audrey was about to mutter some form of see-you-later, Lindsay invited her to join the rest of her friends in the schoolyard. Any familiarity Audrey once had with the English language was momentarily gone. Weren't Lindsay and her friend, Hillary Wright, the awful girls that hurt Gretchen?

"Wait 'til Hill and Jess see your hair. And the color is so gorgeous. I've always wanted to have red hair. Did you know that green is your color?" Lindsay prattled on effortlessly as they approached the hallway of jacket hooks.

Before Audrey could make any reply, she found herself putting her jacket on and walking out the door with Lindsay to the schoolyard. She hated to admit it, but Lindsay was really nice. She couldn't believe it, but it was true. Maybe her friends weren't that bad either.

Walking into the sun, Audrey followed Lindsay up a slight rise where a small group of girls were talking and milling about. She instantly recognized the girls as "the clique," whose members knew everything and dressed the best and always seemed to be understanding some inside joke on the world. Audrey didn't want to go, but Lindsay was able to pull her along just by the force of her dynamic personality.

"Hey, guys, I want you to meet my new friend, Audrey Tabor," announced Lindsay.

With that, all heads turned to Audrey, who was smiling but wishing she could disappear.

All five girls looked at Audrey but barely acknowledged her until a short girl with dark hair said, "Well any friend of Lindsay's is a friend of mine! Totally cool braid, Audrey!"

Once Jessica Morton spoke, a certain indefinable tension in the air seemed to release, allowing the four other group members to extend their greetings, as well.

"Audrey," continued Jessica, "I'm Jessica and this is Hillary, Cassie, and Brianna. We are the 'Style Girls,' and we can make the rest of you look just as cool as your hair. You've got a great start. You're just lucky we found you! Is it true you used to live in Boston?"

"Yes," replied Audrey, overwhelmed by Jessica's take-charge attitude. But how did Jessica know where she came from?

"I love the boutiques on Newbury Street! My mom and I sometimes shop there and then drop in for a dessert at the Taj. Isn't it the best?" interrupted Brianna.

"Well, I —" started Audrey.

"Oh, tell me you don't adore the chocolate torte!" gushed Hillary.

It was clear that Audrey was tongue-tied, when Jessica reprimanded the group.

"Will all of you stupid big mouths stop talking! Audrey can't even speak!" Jessica whispered to Audrey, "Sorry, sometimes my girls have no manners."

The group became more quiet. Hillary, Brianna, and Cassie entered into a private conversation, and Lindsay, Jessica, and Audrey remained a separate group. Audrey watched Lindsay as she adjusted her belt, and tightened and smoothed down her already perfect ponytail. When Jessica put her arm across Audrey's shoulder as if they were old friends, Audrey couldn't help but notice passing glances from other girls in the schoolyard. It made her feel important.

As the school bell rang, Jessica said, "Lindsay will take down your phone number when you guys get back to class, O.K., Audrey? It'll be so fun to do stuff together! And keep the braid! It's great!"

With a smile, Audrey rejoined the reluctant throng of students as they made their way back to afternoon writing projects and math worksheets.

CHAPTER

11

There are plenty of acquaintances in the world,
but very few real friends.
– *Chinese Proverb*

Later that day, Audrey called Gretchen to see how she was feeling. She hadn't seen her friend in five days and was deeply missing her. She missed the laughter at lunch and recess and the easygoing conversations about shared feelings and general observations. She also missed ending the school day at the Harts' house instead of in the boring after-school Kids Club. She was wondering if Gretchen felt the same way — or maybe she was feeling too horrible to care…

"Hi, Gretch, how ya doing? Any better?" asked Audrey.

Gretchen's voice sounded soft and weak, but happy for the phone call.

"Oh, I'm better, I guess. I can't believe I'm saying this, but I'd rather be in school! I've been so sick that I haven't even been watching T.V. My mom has had to help me get to the bathroom because I've been getting dizzy when I stand. I'm feeling a little better today, though — until I took a look at the homework you gave to my mom! Thanks a lot, Audrey!"

Audrey giggled, "Don't mention it, Gretch. You might as well suffer along with the rest of us!"

"So what's new at school?" asked Gretchen. "Anything new and interesting? Any good gossip? Anybody accidentally trip Jessica Morton in the hall? Ha, ha!"

Audrey produced a laugh that she hoped sounded genuine. She and Gretchen had been directing these kinds of jokes at the "the girls" ever since Gretchen confided her story to Audrey. This was the first time Audrey ever pretended with a friend to feel something she didn't completely feel.

Sidestepping the subject of Jessica, Audrey replied, "You haven't missed anything at all. Same old thing. Arnold got in trouble for writing on the hall bulletin board. And he's so dumb he wrote his own name! Big surprise, right?"

The story made Gretchen laugh so hard she coughed, and then answered, "Can you imagine what he must be like at home? He must drive his family crazy!" After a few seconds of silence, Gretchen continued, "So, do you miss me? Have you been sitting with anyone at lunch?"

Audrey answered in her best matter-of-fact voice, "Oh, Keisha and Micah, basically. They're kind of fun. And, yes," she added emphatically, "I do miss you, Gretch! When are you coming back?"

"Not 'til Monday, Aud. I'm barely able to walk around now, and the doctor says I need two or three more days to get well, and that's the weekend, anyway. But I'm not contagious, so maybe you can visit? I'm getting really bored, and my brothers are noisy and stupid. Especially Eric, who's really mad that his dumb friend couldn't come over to play video games. Actually, Mark's been kind of cute — asking me if I want a drink of water and stuff. My mom has had to drag him out of the room so he wouldn't catch anything."

Audrey was thinking that Mark was a lot like Mattie — pesty but cute. But most importantly, she was thinking that she wanted to see her friend more than anything, and was very excited about the prospect of spending time with her. Mulling over her schedule, she replied, "Well, while you're out sick, I'm stuck in the after-school program 'til about six o'clock every night. My mom's been working late. So, then we go home and have dinner and then I have to do my homework. The problem is, I don't think I'll be able to see you 'til maybe Friday after dinner. If not Friday, I'll definitely see you on Saturday. O.K.?"

The girls made tentative plans. Gretchen asked a couple of questions about the math homework. Audrey told Gretchen about how her cousin Beth taught her to make a French braid. Then they said goodbye.

As Audrey hung up the phone on the kitchen wall and turned to go up to her room, her mother asked, "So, honey, how is poor Gretchen feeling? It sounds like she's doing better."

Audrey related the conversation to her mother, mentioning the part about her maybe making a visit before the weekend. Mrs. Tabor agreed that Friday looked like a good day, because she wouldn't have to do homework that night. So, Friday it was. Audrey would let Gretchen know.

While she climbed the stairs slowly to her room, knowing that she couldn't put off her doing her homework any longer, the phone rang. Her mother answered, and called her to the kitchen.

"Audrey," whispered her mother, phone against her chest, "it's someone by the name of Lindsay."

Audrey's heart skipped a beat and continued to beat like a jackhammer on cement. She tried to look and sound nonchalant when she answered her mother but inwardly, could not believe that someone like Lindsay Brentoff would ever really call her — plain old Audrey Tabor. Maybe, she thought, the call was just for homework help. No, Lindsay was smart and never seemed to have difficulty with stuff like that. Audrey was having trouble finding reasons for the call.

Trying earnestly to keep her voice steady and even-sounding, Audrey replied, "Oh, she's a girl in my class. We talk sometimes."

Audrey took the phone from her mother, breathed a long, slow, silent, deep mass of air, and began, "Hi, Lindsay, how are you?"

"Hi, Aud. Listen, Hill and I were wondering if you might

like to join us Friday after school at Jessica's house. You know, kind of hang out, throw in a dvd, cook up some pasta, or something. We usually have sort of a Friday thing going. This week it's at Jessica's, but we rotate from week to week. Give the maid a break, you know?"

Audrey wondered if that "maid" part was a joke, but decided not to ask. She also wondered if she had been suddenly transported from the world she had known to some unnamed place. Could this impossibly wonderful invitation be happening to her? But most of all, could she manage to unravel her knotted tongue enough to avoid tripping over the words, "Thanks, I'd love to"?

Because Mrs. Tabor did not know these girls, the invitation needed some discussion. Audrey enthusiastically thanked Lindsay and reluctantly told her she would call her right back after she checked with her mom.

Her mother began, "You know, Audrey, I don't like allowing you to go to the house of someone I've never met. I don't know anything about this girl or her friends, and particularly, her family. What are they like? Who will be home with all of you? Where do they live? These are very important issues, and a matter of your well being."

Audrey was feeling panicked. How could she turn down this invitation? She would be so embarrassed, and maybe they'd be upset and never invite her again. How could she say, "My mother won't let me"? They'd think she was a baby. How could she convince her mother that it was O.K. to go?

"Mom," she began slowly, trying not to whine, "Lindsay and her friends are really nice, and everyone in school knows them. Lindsay and Jessica are two of the smartest kids in school. They said they liked my French braid that you helped me make the other day. And anyway, I really really want to go over Friday."

Mrs. Tabor stuffed the last dinner dish into the dishwasher and, leaning against the counter, silently sorted out the options. Audrey watched her mother, holding her breath and trusting that the outcome would be in her favor.

"O.K., Audrey, here's my answer," said her mother. "Invite Lindsay and her friends over for dinner either tomorow or Thursday night. Then we'll see."

Audrey's eyes widened with fear. "You're not going to ask them a million embarrassing questions, are you? I would just die. And what am I supposed to say when I'm inviting them — 'I can't come over 'til my mom checks you out'?"

"Look, Honey, I'm trying to be fair and helpful here, and frankly, it's the only option you've got. And if I could invite their parents, too, I would!"

Audrey's eyes widened in horror, and as she opened her mouth to protest, her mother quickly assured her that the parents would not be part of the invitation.

Mrs. Tabor continued, "Now, you know me better than this. I would never be insulting or embarrassing, and I promise you it will be a pleasant dinner. Why don't you tell them that I thought their invitation was so lovely that I wanted to thank them by having them to dinner. If they think that's strange, then you have my permission to tell them that you have a strange mother. O.K.? Is that fair?"

Audrey silently shrugged.

"And if they say no," continued her mother, "then tell them it's very important to me."

With that, she smiled, grabbed Audrey's face in her hands, and kissed her on the head. "Now call Lindsay back and then do your homework. It's getting late."

As Audrey picked up the phone, her mother said, "Oh, Audrey, weren't you going to see Gretchen Friday evening?"

Audrey stood still, remembering their forgotten conversation. "That's all right," she answered, "I can see Gretchen on Saturday."

She assured herself that this was fine. She would just tell Gretchen that Saturday was an easier day for her. She didn't have to say exactly what was happening on Friday, did she? There was nothing wrong with that. Nothing wrong at all.

CHAPTER

12

Have no friends not equal to yourself.

– Confucius

Calling Lindsay back with her mother's bizarre invitation was the most uncomfortable thing Audrey had ever had to do. She tried to make light of the invitation, but she knew that it must have sounded exactly like what it was — a kind of inspection. Every word she spoke to Lindsay was accompanied by a hard lump in her throat and a heartbeat that she believed was audible. Audrey had a picture in her mind of Lindsay going back to Jessica and Hillary, and of all three of them laughing their heads off over the horrible situation.

Surprisingly, the phone conversation seemed to go quite well, and on Thursday evening at six o'clock the Tabor family was joined by Lindsay, Hillary, and Jessica for a dinner of roast chicken and whipped potatoes.

"I want ice cream!" exclaimed Matthew, as he constructed

a canal out of his gravy and potatoes.

Mrs. Tabor put down her fork, and answered in a deliberate voice, "Mattie, ice cream is for after you eat your dinner. All you have done is build things out of your food. When you make your rivers and mountains disappear, then you can have ice cream."

Audrey rolled her eyes and turned her face away in disgust. As she was about to ask Jessica a question in order to change the subject, Hillary shrieked, "Oh, he's so cute! Isn't Mattie the cutest little kid, Jessica?"

Matthew looked up and scowled. As far as he was concerned, he was not a cute little kid. He was five and in kindergarten. Couldn't these dumb girls tell he wasn't a baby anymore? He knew his alphabet and numbers and he could even read street signs, like "STOP." The one with the blonde ponytail looked almost like she was going to hug him! Yuck!

"I wish I had a little brother or sister. My sister, Gabby, is away in college," said Jessica.

"Oh," replied Mrs. Tabor, "what school is she in?"

"She's at Stanford, and that's in California, so we don't get to see her that often, except at school vacations, but we talk on the computer."

Audrey glanced at her mom, and couldn't help but notice that she looked impressed with Jessica. Actually, when Audrey thought about it, her mom seemed pretty impressed with all the girls throughout dinner. Even her dad had joined the girls in an earlier discussion on town events and services. Jessica informed him about library programs and the building of a new restaurant by the highway. There were lots of "please's" and "thank you's," and both Lindsay and Jessica didn't slouch or keep their elbows on the table, and you could tell they were really smart — especially when the discussion turned to the latest reading assignment and Hillary and Jessica debated opinions on the author's point of view. Even Audrey was impressed; she was still trying to remember which character was which.

Matthew decided to prove how grown up he was by eating his construction site instead of expanding it, which put him in line for the vanilla bean ice cream Mrs. Tabor was beginning to serve.

After dessert, Lindsay offered to help with the dishes while Jessica and Hillary began to remove the plates and glasses from the table. Mrs. Tabor beamed, and insisted that the girls spend some time with one another before the three girls left for home. (After all, it was a school night.) They all headed for Audrey's room.

Audrey stood in the middle of her bedroom while Hillary sat on the rocking chair and Jessica and Lindsay strolled from place to place, inspecting the landscape. Audrey hoped her room didn't look too geeky for Jessica's taste. She began wondering what Jessica's room was like.

"Your parents loved me, Audrey, especially when I

talked about helping my mom with the chores. They love stuff like that!" boasted Lindsay.

"Cool rug! Your room is cute, Aud," Jessica said, as she looked at little ceramic boxes and hand lotions on Audrey's bureau. She picked up Audrey's "Friends Forever" poem, and quickly put it down when she spied a silver bracelet with a heart charm lying on the desk. Audrey was feeling uneasy, like the way she felt in school sometimes when she was afraid her work wasn't good enough. But Jessica had called her rug "cool," so that was a good sign, she thought.

"Hey, where'd you get this great bracelet?" asked Jessica as she quickly slipped it on her wrist.

Lindsay got up from the rocking chair to see the piece of jewelry that had taken all of Jessica's attention. Hillary dropped a copy of *Little Women* on the floor by the bookcase and joined the girls.

The bracelet had been a gift from Audrey's Aunt Bette and Uncle Frank on their return from a vacation in Montreal a year before, and it was one of her most prized possessions. At this particular moment, she was sorry she hadn't taken the time to put it back in its little case.

"Let me try it on after you, Jess," said Lindsay impatiently, as she sidled up to her friend.

"Hey, cool!" added Hillary, looking on.

Jessica held up her wrist to the light of Audrey's desk lamp, noticing the engraving on the back of the silver heart.

"Your aunt and uncle, huh?"

"Yeah, they're the best," replied Audrey, hoping that they'd get tired of talking about the bracelet and put it down.

"Come on, lemme try. My wrist is way more delicate that yours, anyway," whined Lindsay.

"O.K., baby," returned Jessica. "Give me a chance to get it off, will ya? Audrey, see what a big idiot baby Lindsay is?"

As Jessica attempted to open the chain, Lindsay prematurely pulled on the bracelet, and the clasp broke.

The two girls continued to argue with each other, each one blaming the other and neither one apologizing to Audrey, who stood frozen and speechless.

When Jessica looked up and saw a very distressed Audrey, she realized what they had done and immediately offered heartfelt apologies. Lindsay was absent-mindedly adjusting her already perfect ponytail when Jessica poked her in the ribs and gave her a stern look.

"Oh, yeah, I'm sorry, Audrey, about your bracelet," Lindsay murmured, and quickly returned to inspecting her hair and clothing. Hillary had turned her back and was over at the bookcase again, scanning Audrey's books to keep clear of the bracelet situation.

Jessica then said they would pay for the repair and insisted that Audrey give her the bill. And the two added a little hug for Audrey as part of the peace offering.

Just then, Audrey's mom called up the stairs that Audrey

had a phone call. Closing her bedroom door behind her, Audrey stood at the landing, asking who was on the phone.

"It's Milly," announced her mom with a smile. "And tell the girls that Jessica's dad has pulled into the driveway."

After several seconds, Audrey replied, "Ask her if I can call her back, O.K.?"

"Audrey, I think it would be nice if you took the call, don't you think? Even for a couple of minutes."

"Tell her I'll call her back as soon as I can. I promise."

With that, Mrs. Tabor sighed as she made her way back to the family room, and Audrey quickly returned to her guests.

"So, anyhow, Aud," said Jessica, after hearing Mrs. Tabor's announcement, "we gotta go. It's getting late, and I've got school stuff. Do you think you're on for Friday night, my place?"

"Are you kidding?" laughed Lindsay. "After the way her mom loved us? No *problemo*, right Audrey?" Lindsay gave a thumbs up sign to Audrey as she tossed the silver bracelet over onto the desk.

"Yeah, great! I'll be there!" Audrey replied ecstatically.

With her heart tharumping wildly in her chest, Audrey smiled widely as the girls sailed down the stairs, hair flying behind them. She faintly heard them say "thank you" to her mother as a storm door slammed.

Audrey found her heart bracelet lying beside her "Friend" poem. Upon close inspection she saw that there was indeed a pull in the clasp. Just as she set the bracelet down again and started to walk away, she noticed a large diagonal scratch across the glass — directly over the poem and the two girls sitting on the bench.

CHAPTER

13

A man should keep his friendship in constant repair.

– Samuel Johnson

On Friday morning, Audrey's alarm went off at the usual hour of seven o'clock, but Audrey had been awake since 5:48 a.m. She knew this because she read her digital clock after tossing around in bed and being unable to return to sleep. It was still dark when she awoke and the house was without sound and movement, and she was very frustrated that she couldn't make herself get back to sleep. She tried lying still with her eyes closed; she tried thinking of all the movies that had a color in the title; she tried thinking peaceful thoughts of gardens and beaches and windchimes in the summer breeze. But the harder she tried the more wide awake she became, and pretty soon all she thought about was the evening's invitation to Jessica's house with the "Style Girls." What should she wear? Did she even have anything that could measure up to their cool clothes? How should she wear her hair? Lindsay really loved her French braid; could she get her mom to make it for her? What about jewelry?

When Audrey thought about jewelry, she remembered, with a sinking feeling, her broken heart bracelet. Before she had gone to bed the night before, she had placed the bracelet in her top bureau drawer, underneath her underwear. She didn't want to look at it, and didn't want to tell her mother, but she wasn't sure why. Lindsay and Jessica — especially Jessica — were really nice about the accident. Jessica even offered to pay for the repair. But Audrey knew she would be too embarrassed to present her with the bill.

Nursing the beginning of a stomach ache, Audrey got up and stood in front of her closet as if she were looking at her clothes for the very first time. Normally, she would pull down a pair of jeans from her closet shelf — maybe the flowered ones, maybe plain — and find a T-shirt and white socks from her dresser. And, finally, with a pair of sneakers, she'd be dressed and ready for breakfast. But this morning, everything seemed ugly and drab, and between her clothing dilemma and her stomach ache, Audrey was feeling unhappy. And to make matters worse, she suddenly remembered that she hadn't called Gretchen to reschedule her visit for Saturday. She had to make up some believable excuse, because she knew she couldn't tell Gretchen about her invitation to Jessica's. Reluctantly deciding on the flowered jeans and a yellow tee, Audrey put a yellow covered band around her ponytail, gathered her books from her desk, and went downstairs. With all these issues swimming in her head, Audrey sat herself down at the kitchen table, and stared vacantly at the wall clock.

Mrs. Tabor was upstairs helping Matthew dress, and Mr. Tabor was already seated at the table, eating cereal, bananas, and toast and reading the local morning news. When Audrey pulled her chair out and noisily threw herself down into it, Mr. Tabor put down his paper and looked up.

"Morning, Audrey, Shmaudrey! What's new besides New York, New Jersey, and New England?"

Usually, her dad's overused jokes made Audrey laugh and say something silly or sarcastic in return. But this morning's joke got no response at all.

Leaning forward slightly, Audrey's dad responded, "Hey, Funny Face, what's going on? Do you have your ears turned off?"

Audrey was startled to see her dad staring at her expectantly, and realized she'd been so deep in thought that she hadn't heard much of what he had said.

"Oh, sorry, Dad. I was just thinking about stuff in school. I guess I wasn't paying attention."

"Well," said Mr. Tabor, as he took the last bite out of his toast, "you missed my best material."

"Yeah," answered Audrey, with a smirk, "it was probably the same old joke. Mattie's starting to repeat your jokes. I can't believe it!"

"Matthew is a man of discriminating taste, my dear girl. And with that, I have to leave for work." Mr. Tabor rose from his seat, walked around to where Audrey was sitting and kissed her on the head.

"Daddy?" started Audrey.

"What, kiddo?" answered her father as he grabbed his sports jacket and keys.

"Oh, nothing. Have great day, Dad," said Audrey, as she sat back in her chair, debating whether she should attempt to eat breakfast.

As Tom Tabor called goodbye to his wife, whom he thought was upstairs with Matthew, Alice appeared suddenly in the hall walking toward the kitchen. After startling each other, they kissed goodbye and briefly discussed plans for the evening.

Mr. Tabor left for the office and now Audrey was sharing the kitchen with her mom and brother.

"Audrey," said her mother, while emptying the dish drainer of salad tongs and measuring cups, "why aren't you eating breakfast? You'll be late if you don't start eating soon. Mattie, don't take your shoes off again! Audrey, Cheerios or Rice Krispies?"

Audrey managed to swallow most of her Rice Krispies and orange juice, although she hardly remembered consuming any of it. As she waited for the bus, she formulated in her mind what she would tell Gretchen and worried that her clothes and her hair didn't have the right "look." They called themselves the "Style Girls," and Audrey was feeling conspicuously unstylish for the first time in her life. Not that she ever felt particularly in style; she just never thought about it at all. Now suddenly she was noticing other girls and how they dressed and acted. Well, she could ask her mom if she could get some new clothes. But what would be good? Lindsay or Jessica might help her with that. Wouldn't they? They seemed to like her. Didn't they?

The bus ride was pretty much like breakfast — a big blur. Before Audrey knew it (or didn't know it), she was hanging her backpack on one of the hall hooks. As she turned toward the classroom door, Lindsay put her arm around her shoulder and said hello.

"Boy, Audrey, you look like you lost your best friend! Tonight's gonna be great. We'll see you at recess, and you'll join us at our table for lunch, O.K., girlfriend?"

As Lindsay walked away, Audrey noticed her jean skirt with pink stitching and pink sandals and matching belt. Her shirt was blue with lace trim on the sleeves and collar. She was wearing a pink headband and her hair was perfect. And she had called Audrey "girlfriend" and invited her to their lunch table. Audrey felt special.

After math class, Lindsay accompanied Audrey out to the girls' special recess place on the little hill in back of the school. Since the group began meeting there last year, the rest of the school population accepted the location as the Style Girls' turf and stayed away. It had a great vantage point; anyone standing on the knoll could look down at everything.

When Lindsay arrived with Audrey, Cassie and Brianna were deep in conversation and seemed to be comparing nail polish or something on their hands. They both looked up as Lindsay approached.

"Hi, Linds," said Cassie. "The nail polish Brianna and I bought last night is to die for. I swear, orange!" With that, Cassie and Brianna glanced up at Audrey. They said nothing, but strolled off a little way down the hill, talking quietly together.

Jessica and Hillary joined Lindsay and Audrey, and all waited, it seemed, for Jessica to speak, but Jessica turned quietly to them and said, almost in a whisper, "We're on for tonight, right?"

The girls nodded, and Lindsay gave a thumbs up and patted Audrey on the back.

Jessica continued, "Great. Just us. We don't want that loser, Cassie, ruining everything. And if Brianna insists on hanging out with Miss Loser, then she's a loser, too. Right?"

Hillary and Lindsay agreed, and Jessica looked toward Audrey and smiled. "We'll explain everything tonight at my place, Audrey. Six o'clock sharp, girls, and bring your appetites."

Hillary, Lindsay, and Jessica spent the remainder of

recess discussing jewelry and hair, and shared a few laughs over Blossom Hill's famously geeky dressers. Soon it was time to return to class.

The remainder of the school day went relatively well. Audrey, as usual, had read her ten-page assignment on the Industrial Revolution and answered the questions at the end of the section. She also read more of *The Secret Garden*, her independent reading selection.

"Complete your homework, and the rest is easy," her mom always told her. The cliché would have proven true today, except for assorted distractions. Audrey knew that Lowell, Massachusetts was the site of the Industrial Revolution, but distractedly answered, "Littleton." During a class game of "Name that Fact," Audrey was conversing in sign language with Lindsay, across the room, and so, missed her fact. During silent reading, Audrey's mind kept zigzagging between Gretchen and her exciting invitation to Jessica's house (tinged with the agony of what to wear). The chapter would have to be read again.

Dismissal came mercifully at three o'clock, and Audrey made her way with the after-school crowd to the cafeteria. Gretchen was still absent, so Audrey had had to wait until later for her mom to pick her up. Today was already feeling like the longest afternoon of her life.

As she approached the double doorway to the increasingly noisy cafeteria, Lindsay and Jessica called out to her.

"Hey, Dandelion!" called Jessica in a sing-songy voice. When she received no response, she repeated the name, this time louder and accompanied by Lindsay.

"Yoohoo! Dandelion!" they sang in giggling unison.

This time, Audrey turned to see what the nonsense was all about, and discovered in surprise that it was all about her.

"Hey, silly, we're talking to you! We decided that that yellow shirt makes you look like a dandelion," said Jessica. "We were thinking that maybe one day we should all decide to come to school dressed like garden flowers!"

"Yeah," continued Lindsay. "Like I could be a red rose and maybe Jessie could be a blue hydrangea!"

"And Cassie could be a ragweed," smirked Jessica with a self-satisfied grin. The two girls looked at each other and then at Audrey, drawing her into their joke with a conspiratorial laugh.

At first Audrey wasn't sure if the girls were making fun of her yellow shirt or complimenting her on it. But when they included her in the ragweed joke, she figured they were being friendly toward her. It was just so hard to tell sometimes with girls who were so cool and seemed to know so many things and feel so comfortable about everything. It was hard to know when to laugh along, or speak, or be silent.

As Audrey smiled in agreement, the girls reminded her again about the invitation for that evening, and turned to leave the building. Audrey watched Lindsay's perfect blonde ponytail bop back and forth and up and down as she and Jessica glided down the hallway toward the exit door and the waiting buses. Lindsay's pink sandals matched her belt to perfection. As she stared after her, Audrey wondered how many pairs of shoes Lindsay must own in order to match so many outfits. There was no way Audrey's mom would ever agree to buying that many pairs of shoes. And Jessica always had beautiful bracelets and earrings. Today, her blue mini-skirt was set off by a silver and blue ankle bracelet — the first girl at Blossom Hill School she had seen wearing one.

As Audrey took a seat in the "caf," she glanced at her white sneakers and baggy jeans and daydreamed of bracelets, sandals, and mini-skirts.

CHAPTER

14

We are all travellers in the wilderness of this world,
and the best that we find in our travels is an honest friend.

– Robert Louis Stevenson

"…but I'll definitely see you tomorrow. O.K., Gretch?"

Audrey, who called Gretchen directly upon returning home, was finishing her explanation regarding the postponement of their visit. She had told her that Friday had turned out to be not so good because her cousin Beth was coming over.

"That's all right. Saturday will be better anyway, because we'll have more time, and I'll probably feel even better by then," answered Gretchen in her usual understanding manner. "So, how is your pal these days?"

"Who?" replied a startled Audrey.

"Beth, silly! Are you half-asleep?" teased Gretchen. "I thought I was the tired one!"

"Oh, yeah — Beth. She's as fine as ever. So, I guess I

gotta go, but I'll be over tomorrow, Gretch!" said Audrey absentmindedly.

They said their goodbyes, and after Audrey hung up the phone, she looked up to find her mother standing in the middle of the kitchen staring at her quizzically. She had come home early today, especially to pick up Audrey in time so that she would be ready for her evening at Jessica's house.

"Audrey, why did you lie to Gretchen about tonight?" asked her mom softly.

Audrey suddenly felt like she was just caught cheating on a math test and needed to explain her behavior — quickly.

"Well, I didn't want to hurt Gretchen's feelings and make her think that she was being replaced, or something," replied Audrey rapidly.

Mrs. Tabor listened to Audrey's explanation, let several seconds of silence pass, and, as Audrey looked at her mother, then down at her sneakers, and then back up at her mother again, Mrs. Tabor spoke thoughtfully and slowly.

"Why would she feel that way? Is Gretchen being replaced?"

The question was like one of those surprise attacks during a game when you're dribbling the ball and somebody comes out of nowhere and steals the ball away.

"No, Mom!" Audrey was in genuine disbelief that her mother could suggest that she would ever want to replace Gretchen with anybody. "I love Gretchen! I would never do that to her! I just didn't want her to feel bad, that's all. Really."

Audrey was genuine in her feelings and taken aback by her mother's suggestion. And yet, she knew she'd lied to her friend. Furthermore, she knew deep down that the lie was told not only for Gretchen's benefit, but for her own, as well. It was all something she did not want to think about, not now. Mrs. Tabor reluctantly accepted her daughter's reassurances, deciding against any further discussion.

Audrey turned quickly and ran upstairs to change — into what, she didn't know. Taking rapid stock of her wardrobe, she saw sneakers, jeans, tees, special clothes for holidays and events, but, on the whole, nothing very impressive, nothing cool. Remembering that the girls seemed to like her yellow shirt, she decided to just leave on what she had been wearing. Audrey grabbed her canvas bag of hair things and cds and favorite dvds and flew down the stairs, meeting her mom by the back door. Her mom made sure she had her directions to Jessica's house, and together they made their way to the car.

As they drove along toward Jessica's neighborhood, the landscape underwent a definite transformation. Little ranches and cozy colonials in close, tricycle-strewn neighboring lots gradually gave way to formality on a grand scale. Imposing houses adorned by stone walls and iron gates; three- and four-car garages; pillared entryways; spectacular carpets of lawn nurtured by elaborate underground watering systems. And each domicile set apart from its neighbor by sizeable acreage and lush vegetation. It amazed both Alice and Audrey Tabor that this world existed in Greenwood Springs.

Mrs. Tabor pulled up to 37 Berry Hill Drive, a rose-beige, maroon-shuttered, three-story edifice with a four-car garage and a Mercedes convertible parked in the driveway. As Mrs. Tabor began to open her side of the car, Audrey quickly stopped her.

"Mom, I'm not a baby. You don't have to bring me to the door!"

"I just wanted to thank Jessica's mother for inviting you. I'm not treating you like a baby. But if it makes you uncomfortable, then I'll just wait in the car until I know you're inside, O.K.? Now, remember, I don't want to pick you up any later than ten o'clock."

"Thanks, Mom," replied Audrey, as she leaned over and gave her mother a kiss.

Audrey took her bag and walked up the winding brick walk to the massive maroon double front door. As she stood admiring the lush floral arrangement that sat in the stone basket on the landing, a voice called to her from the direction of the driveway.

"Audrey, dear, come in through the kitchen."

When Audrey approached the driveway, she came upon her mother conversing with a woman who had to be Mrs. Morton. She was dressed all in white — white jacket, white sweater and shorts, and white sneakers and socks — and she was holding a tennis racquet. Lying against the neck of her sweater was a gold chain that sparkled brilliantly. Her dark hair was pulled back in some kind of elaborate configuration at the nape of her neck. She looked up and saw Audrey.

"Oh, Audrey, so nice to meet you," said Mrs. Morton. "Jessie has been speaking about you, and is so looking forward to having you over. I was just telling your mother that normally I would love to have her in for tea, but I'm dashing off to play some tennis with friends." She turned to Alice Tabor and said, "Next time, Mrs. Tabor, I promise."

Audrey's mother replied, "Oh, please don't apologize for your schedule. And do call me Alice."

"And please call me Julia."

While Audrey approached the side entrance she cringed as she heard her mother ask, "Oh, by the way, Julia, if you're leaving, who will be with the girls?"

Getting into her Mercedes, Julia Morton replied, "Don't worry, Alice. The girls will be with Anita, our maid. She's quite responsible."

Jessica's mother pulled out of the driveway with Audrey's mom following. And Audrey stepped into a world she had never seen outside of a movie or T.V. show.

CHAPTER

15

The object of love is to serve, not to win.

– *Woodrow Wilson*

Audrey tapped lightly on the open door. She could hear the thumping of music coming from someplace within. When no one came to the door, she decided to walk in cautiously. Before her stood a kitchen three times bigger than her own, with a dark blue and white check floor and a vast array of white cabinets set off by counters that matched the deep blue of the floor. There was a little garden growing upon shelves built into a wide window. The window overlooked the rolling blanket of green that was the Mortons' back yard. Under this window sat a set of blue chairs and a white table majestically adorned with a humongous, shiny red bowl of multicolored fruit. Appliances, large and small, for uses she could not imagine, were situated everywhere.

Conscious again of the music playing, Audrey wondered

whether it was coming from the radio or from Jessica's cd player. It had suddenly occurred to her that the girls probably didn't realize that she was in the house. Deciding to look for Jessica and Lindsay by following the sound of the music, Audrey walked into a very large formal dining room. She couldn't help but stop to admire the gleaming wood floor with its thick floral rug. Looking up, she saw a set of shuttered bay windows that faced the front lawn. The blue and white striped cushion on its window seat matched the upholstery on all ten dark wood chairs. The long, graceful curtains had a floral pattern similar to that of the rug.

Audrey wondered how people were able to do that — match things so well, the way they look in fancy magazines. She thought about her family's living room, with the blue sofa, the bamboo coffee table with the green top, and the rug in different shades of brown, one end table that was glass and one that was wood, and the books in the bookcase that sat upright, sideways, and slanted on the white-painted shelves. She thought of their kitchen, that was barely big enough to hold a table and four chairs, and of the window that held a view of their back yard — and just about everyone else's — barking dogs and crying babies included. It's not that she didn't like her house. She loved it, but this place suddenly began to make her wonder what Jessica must have thought of her home the evening she came for dinner. It made her wonder what Jessica saw in her, and why she was inviting her into her circle of friends.

As she was pondering so many things, Lindsay appeared suddenly at the dining room doorway. She was barefoot and model slender in tight jeans and a pink top. Her hair was in a pink headband and hung loosely, nearly to her waist. Pulling her hair away from the side of her face, she displayed a silver earring of moon and stars that dangled to the middle of her neck.

"Hi, Audrey! We thought we heard something downstairs, but we weren't sure. Jess had her music playing kind of loud, I guess." As Lindsay noticed Audrey's canvas bag, she remarked, "What's in the bag?"

Audrey was distracted by the surroundings, her meandering thoughts, and now by Lindsay's cool beauty, and so she did not respond.

"Hey, Earth to Audrey! Come in, Audrey Tabor!" teased Lindsay as she waved her hands in front of Audrey's face.

Audrey embarrassedly pulled herself back into the moment. "Oh, I'm sorry, Lindsay. I guess my mind was someplace else! What did you ask me?"

"The bag, Aud. What did you bring?"

As Audrey was about to run down the list of items, Lindsay interrupted, "You know what? You can show us later. Come on with me. We're up in Jessie's room. She didn't come down because she's in a real snit. She lost one of her bracelets and her mom won't buy her a replacement. Hillary's on her way, and if Brianna doesn't come tonight, Jessie's going to be really upset."

As Lindsay led Audrey up the most elegant winding staircase that Audrey had ever seen, she turned to her and said reassuringly, "But she's really happy you came."

Audrey felt as if someone had poured thick liquid sunshine all over her.

———————————

At the top of the stairs, Lindsay turned left and Audrey followed. From here Audrey had a full view of the downstairs entry hall. The floor was made of a white marble tile, and the double front door was trimmed on each side by some kind of fancy glass with a floral design etched in. An umbrella stand, some tall plants, and a table with matching mirror sat at their appointed places. A monstrous and exquisite crystal chandelier presided over all this, hanging majestically from the second floor ceiling — quite close to where Audrey and Lindsay were now standing.

"This house is so beautiful," murmured Audrey, as she stared at the many glass prisms that made up the amazing light fixture.

"Huh? Oh, yeah, it's cool, I suppose," answered Lindsay indifferently as they approached Jessica's bedroom. "Well," she announced, "here we are! The inner sanctum of Jessica Morton! Enter if you dare!" she added with a chuckle.

"Ta da!" sang Lindsay as she opened Jessica's door. "Your

first subject has arrived, your majesty!"

Audrey stepped into a room that was about the size of her family's dining room and kitchen combined — maybe bigger. The bed was queen size (not single like hers and all her other friends' beds). The dresser, bureau, and desk were all painted white and all matched the bed. The walls and thick wall-to-wall carpet were sky blue and the ceiling was painted to look just like a fluffy-clouded sky. Audrey remembered that Milly had always dreamed of having a ceiling like that. Lamps and various accessories were sunshine yellow. Jessica even had a dressing table swathed in a yellow and white skirt and accompanied by a white bench with a yellow cushion. To the left of the yellow padded window seat, sat a beautiful blue-stuffed rocking chair.

It would have been the most gorgeous room Audrey had ever seen except for the fact that nearly all the drawers were sitting opened with clothing hanging out of them, and various and sundry items were strewn everywhere — across the white bedspread, over the arms and seat of the rocking chair, along the window seat. Schoolbooks and notebooks and dozens of magazines were scattered on the floor, as well as dvds, stuffed animals of every variety, and the contents of three emptied jewelry boxes.

"I want my bracelet!" shouted Jessica angrily, as she threw a hairbrush across the room.

Lindsay reminded Jessica that Audrey had walked in.

Jessica looked up and smiled at Audrey. She explained, "My mom and dad gave me this amazing emerald bracelet for my last birthday, and I can't find it. I've looked everywhere, and I don't know how it could have disappeared. It's insured; I don't understand why they don't just get me another one. What's the big deal, anyway? Ya know?"

Audrey didn't know, but she nodded her head in agreement anyway.

Lindsay joked, "You probably just misplaced it under all the junk you never put away!"

"Shut up, Lindsay!" retorted Jessica.

This remark shocked and upset Audrey. The Tabors had a rule against speaking those words to each other or to anyone else, for that matter. Audrey swallowed and pretended not to notice.

As Lindsay knelt down to pick up a magazine, Audrey said, "Would you like me to help you look for it, Jessica? I'm pretty good at finding things." (Audrey was actually thinking it would be pretty tough to locate an elephant in this mess.)

"See, Lindsay," snapped Jessica, "some people are nice."

Audrey smiled wanly, feeling rather uncomfortable, when Jessica abruptly changed the subject and suggested they all leave the mess and go down to the family room to pop corn. They also left the mix in the iHome blaring. It was just four-thirty and dinner wouldn't be 'til later, when Mrs. Morton returned from her tennis match.

As they were assembling the bowl, napkins and glasses for drinks, Anita, the family's housekeeper, appeared at the pantry door.

"Jessica, in case you need me for anything, I'll be straightening up in the library."

The library? thought Audrey. What else does this house have, a movie theater?

"Thanks, Anita," answered Jessica, "we're fine. Hillary and Brianna should be here soon."

Audrey, expecting popcorn out of a microwave bag, was wide-eyed when she saw Jessica working an actual popcorn machine like the kind you'd see at theaters and amusement parks.

A few minutes later, Jessica transferred the popcorn into a large bowl that was set on the kitchen counter. Lindsay poured the soda, and all three girls sat themselves down comfortably on the high, red-padded stools.

Lindsay began, "Jess, why don't you fill Aud in on the deal with Cassie and Brianna?"

Shaking salt over the steaming popcorn, Jessica said, "Cassie's out. She's not our friend anymore. For the last month I've been talking about a party I want to have at the club for all my best friends. I was going over how I wanted to decorate it and what I'd wear and what the theme would be and the food. The whole thing. So, you know what that traitor Cassie does?"

Both Lindsay and Jessica looked at Audrey in

expectation. Audrey shook her head, eyes fixed in interest on Jessica.

Jessica continued, "I'll tell you what that big mouth did. She went ahead and told Brianna, who told Hillary, who told a bunch of nobodies I wouldn't waste my time talking to."

Audrey said, "Oh, is that the story that was going around about the big party with the Japanese lanterns and the lobsters?" Audrey felt proud, somehow, that she was able to make a contribution to the gossipy story.

"You see, Linds? Even Audrey knew about it!" Jessica turned to Audrey and added, "It was just an inner circle secret and now it's all ruined. And to make matters worse, Cassie sent out invitations to her own lobster party before I did mine. I told Brianna and Hillary they'd better not go. I know Hillary is loyal to me, but I'm not sure about Brianna. If she shows up tonight, then maybe we can convince her that she'd better stick with Lindsay, Hillary, and me — and, of course, you, Audrey. She'd better, if she knows what's good for her."

As the girls were finishing the last morsels of their snack, Hillary arrived, followed shortly by Brianna. After a few general greetings, the girls moved the party to the family room, located off the kitchen.

As Audrey looked around, she figured that while the Mortons may not have an actual home movie theater, the wide screen T.V. and popcorn machine brought it pretty close. There were even movie posters and framed snapshots of celebrities with writing on them. She even noticed among this collection a photo of Julie Andrews and some guy smiling into the camera. A family member? Maybe even Jessica's dad? It was totally awesome.

After the group settled into the plush red sofas, Jessica got down to business, laying out the rules of friendship for Hillary and Brianna and reminding them about where their loyalties needed to be. Lindsay reminded Brianna of how the two of them had been friends since first grade and how lucky she was to be in the best group in school — the group with the most style, how everyone looked up to the Style Girls as the school leaders, and how they had their own undisputed place on the schoolyard hill.

Hillary readily agreed. Brianna agreed also but tried to defend Cassie's actions.

"I don't think Cassie really meant any harm, you know? I mean she's pretty cool usually. And don't forget," she added smiling, "her family has that unbelievable pool and clubhouse."

"Who cares about her pool? I can take you all to Countryside almost any time I like," barked Jessica.

"What's Countryside?" asked Audrey.

"Oh my God, Audrey! I don't believe you don't know what that is! You really need to get with the program!" exclaimed Hillary.

Jessica interjected, "Leave Audrey alone. She only just moved to Greenwood Springs a few months ago, right, Aud?"

Jessica put her arm around Audrey's shoulders in an apparent display of affection. Hillary apologized. The sudden sting Audrey felt disappeared, and she smiled with relief.

"Countryside Country Club is where my family belongs. That's where my mom plays tennis and my dad plays golf. And a lot of times, we meet other members there for dinner. All through the summer we use the pool and can take guests. That's why we don't have a pool of our own. Who needs a silly pool, like Cassie's family, when you can go to a club like ours?" As Jessica completed her explanation, she shook her dark hair and ran her fingers through the thick waves.

"You'll see, Audrey. We'll have a blast this summer," promised Lindsay. "And," she continued, "You have got great bones, so you'll look fab-u-lous in a bathing suit. With just a few pounds off, you'll look like a model. I took off a few this spring and you can, too!"

"Hey!" said Jessica, "Let's do our nails! I bought Aqua Marine."

Hillary added, "I brought Orange Mist. It's totally cool."

Later that evening, upon Mrs. Morton's return, the freshly polished girls dined on grilled steak, baked potato, and salad, and hot fudge sundaes for dessert. Lindsay declined the dessert and the potato.

Audrey's dad came for her at nine forty-five, and as she made her way toward the kitchen door Lindsay called out, "So Monday you'll join us at our table for lunch, O.K.?"

Audrey's heart did a flip-flop as she answered, "O.K." On the ride home her head was spinning with the evening's experience. She couldn't wait to tell her mom about the beautiful house and her new exciting friends. She really wanted, more than anything, to measure up.

CHAPTER

16

When I have opened my heart to a friend,

I am more myself than ever.

– Thomas Moore

"Hi, Audrey! We've missed having you around," exclaimed Gretchen's mother as Audrey entered the kitchen. They gave each other a big hug.

"Thanks, Mrs. Hart. I've missed you all, too," answered Audrey.

Straight through the white and green kitchen, Audrey saw her friend lying across one of the light green family room sofas. Saturday morning T.V. was yammering. Mark was on the beige rug, legs splayed, back propped up against an oversized pillow which used the front of the other sofa as support. He was mesmerized by a cartoon cat bonking a cartoon mouse on his head. Gretchen was apparently busy with something sitting in her lap. Making her way toward the room, Audrey sidestepped assorted soccer equipment, children's library books, and puzzles and games. The white kitchen table still held the remnants of breakfast — an open Cheerios box, a bowl, empty except for the last puddle of milk and bits of "O"s stuck to the rim, and small dribbles of milk on the table.

"Hey, Gretch!"

"Hey, Aud!"

As Audrey approached the room, Gretchen arose from the sofa. They met mid-point and embraced in a long-lost-friend bear hug. The next several minutes were spent in exclamations of how much they had missed each other. Audrey was glad to see that Gretchen was dressed and noticed how healthy she looked. Gretchen thought Audrey had grown in the week they were separated. Audrey teased Gretchen that her illness made her imagine things, but Gretchen insisted that her pal seemed different — in a good way, she assured her.

"What were you doing there on the sofa before I came in?" asked Audrey.

"Oh, being sick is really boring. My mom wouldn't let me watch T.V. all day, and only a few videos. So, I've been doing some drawing and stuff. That's all."

"Can I see?"

Gretchen hesitated. "You have to promise not to laugh. I really mean it," she pleaded. "If you laugh I'll be so embarrassed, I'll just die."

Audrey assured Gretchen in her most genuine best friend voice that she would never ever make fun of her in a million years, and pleaded to see her picture.

Gretchen retrieved a large white drawing tablet, and holding the front tightly to her chest in a last hesitating moment, turned it around so that Audrey could view it.

Audrey nearly lost her balance when she saw what her friend had created. It was a drawing of a girl sitting by a window and looking sadly at trees and birds and rain. She looked lonely. It was so expertly drawn, with such emotion, that it took Audrey's breath away. She said nothing.

"You don't like it. I'm sorry, I shouldn't have shown it to you," said Gretchen sadly.

Audrey turned to her friend and began to speak deliberately and slowly. "Gretchen, how long have you been able to do this? I've never seen anything like this. Do you have other pictures?"

"Then, you like it?" asked Gretchen softly.

"Gretch, you're like a regular, real artist — like the pictures we see in museums and high school art shows." Gretchen shook her head in disagreement, but Audrey would not be silenced. "No, this drawing makes me cry," she reiterated, grabbing Gretchen by the arms. "It's so beautiful."

Gretchen explained, "I've been drawing for a while. I draw when I'm bored or sad or angry. I started last year. Some people write; I guess I draw." She self-consciously twisted a clump of rumpled hair while she spoke. In a quiet and careful way she added, "I have more in my room. Wanna see?"

For the next hour, Audrey was flabbergasted and struck nearly speechless by the collection of accomplished and heartbreakingly expressive drawings that her friend had created. She felt as though she had been taken through some secret door. One drawing depicted a laughing girl in a back yard swing; another showed the same girl smiling, wearing a flowered hat; still another displayed the girl sadly sitting in a chair holding a closed book. There were others of trees and houses and flowers set in containers. When the girls were finished looking over the work, Audrey watched Gretchen as she carefully put back the pages in a box that she kept in a corner of her closet.

Audrey stayed for lunch, and all through the meal she felt special and grateful that Gretchen had chosen to share her secret with her. But she had to find some way to convince her that her talent needed to be shared with other people as well. It was something she'd think about for another time.

The day progressed with school talk, movie talk, and favorite teen star talk. And then Gretchen noticed Audrey's painted nails.

"Wow, blue and orange nail polish! That's so weird! You never wore that before!"

Looking down at the painted reminder of her evening with the Style Girls, Audrey smiled back at Gretchen and mumbled, "Uh huh."

"Did Beth do that yesterday?"

It took Audrey a few seconds to remember the excuse she gave Gretchen about visiting her cousin Friday evening. "Oh, yeah. Beth and I were fooling around, you know." Changing the subject she added, "She had a date for the Spring Dance a week ago. I saw his picture; he's really cute."

"You're lucky to have Beth as a cousin. She's seems really nice."

Audrey looked up at the clock in the family room, and was privately thankful that it was four o'clock and time to go. She was feeling very uncomfortable with the present conversation.

As she was about to leave, Gretchen said, "Wait a minute. I'll be right back."

She ran down the hall toward her bedroom, returning a minute later with a large white paper.

"Here, Audrey. I want you to have this."

It was the drawing of the girl at the window that Gretchen had most recently completed — the picture that moved Audrey to tears. It moved her even more to think that her friend would give it to her.

"Thank you so much, Gretch. I don't know what to say. It isn't even my birthday!" She hugged her friend. Both girls laughed.

As Audrey stepped out the kitchen door, Gretchen called, "Hey, Audrey, you're my best friend!"

Audrey answered, "Me too, you!"

CHAPTER

17

He who throws away a friend
is as bad as he who throws away his life.

– *Sophocles*

On Monday both Audrey and Gretchen were thrilled to be reunited. It had felt so strange for Audrey to look over at Gretchen's seat and not have her there to smile at or to share some silly classroom episode. Because they tended to think alike, at times, both girls had to be careful not to look at each other or they would begin to giggle uncontrollably. One such experience had landed them in the principal's office four weeks earlier.

Mrs. Antonelli was organizing the materials needed for her math lesson while the class was quietly reviewing the early morning math problems. Gretchen cleared her throat twice and Audrey looked up to see her friend smiling and making small gestures toward Douglas Baers, who was sitting at the opposite corner of the room.

Douglas put very little effort into any task, unless it involved bathroom humor and burping. He and Arnold Peters had once competed to see who could speak the longest sentence-burp. It was considered an impressive competition among a good many boys, and a topic of disgust among all the girls. Today Douglas was keeping himself happily occupied by picking his nose, without benefit of tissue.

At Gretchen's insistence, Audrey looked over at Douglas in horror. She immediately looked back at Gretchen, and when their eyes locked they started to giggle. But the harder they tried to stop the stronger their giggles became. The second glance at Douglas was the last straw, and now they both lost complete control, clutching their stomachs, crying, and, finally, laughing out loud. When Mrs. Antonelli looked up half the class was fully distracted from their work, attempting to figure out what was so funny.

By the time the girls sat down in the principal's office their fit of laughter had just about subsided — as long as they avoided looking at each other.

That visit to the principal's office had made Gretchen and Audrey's reunion dramatically complete, but now that Lindsay and her friends were in the picture, things needed to be worked out. Audrey was wrong in not telling Gretchen about her new friends. All week she had tried to ignore the truth of this, but she couldn't ignore it anymore. She knew that she should have explained things to Gretchen during her Saturday visit, but she didn't know how. During spelling, Audrey was remembering what Gretchen told her about how badly Hillary had treated her. But Lindsay and Jessica were so nice. Maybe Hillary had changed. There had to be some way to make everyone friends again. Besides, she already accepted their offer to join them for lunch — an unbelievable invitation. Why couldn't she bring Gretchen along? There was no reason they wouldn't want her, was there? Audrey was imagining Gretchen and the girls eating lunch and hanging out on the hill every day. She was even fantasizing about a great summer with the whole group — fixing each other's hair, shopping downtown, swimming. With a little effort it could happen. She was sure of it.

At 10:45 a.m., the class put aside their work for morning recess, and Audrey looked up to find Lindsay smiling at her and waving discreetly. The girls were expecting her to join them on their spot, and Gretchen was expecting that she and Audrey would get their jackets and walk out together as they had been doing every day for months. Audrey ran up quickly to Gretchen and told her that she had something she had to do and could Gretchen wait for her outside? After Gretchen cheerily left, Audrey grabbed Lindsay before she also left the building.

"Hi, Lindsay!" Audrey was arranging and rearranging

her thoughts. "Um, well, you know, Gretchen and I always do recess and lunch together and she's waiting for me outside. But I really want to join you guys, and, um, I was wondering if Gretchen could join us, too. She'll be all alone, and I wouldn't want that to happen. She's my friend, you know?"

Lindsay looked mildly annoyed and remained silent for what seemed to Audrey to be a million years. As Audrey's heart pounded, Lindsay replied, "Well, you can bring her, but I'm not guaranteeing anything. We'll see how it goes with Jessica. She's not our type, you know. I don't think she'll fit in."

"Oh, but Gretchen's great. Really! She's funny and talented," replied Audrey hurriedly, nearly tripping over tongue. Her voice was shaky and her mouth felt dry, as if she were delivering a report in front of an entire classroom.

Lindsay said they would see each other outside, and Audrey quickly ran to find Gretchen. She found her by the side of the building, under the art room windows, where they usually hung out. Here, finally, she began to explain the previous week's experience. She worked hard at describing the group as friendly, supportive, fun, and exciting. She worked hard at stressing how much Gretchen meant to her. She worked hard at making her feel included in the clique.

"I'm sorry I didn't tell you last week. I guess I didn't want to make you upset," said Audrey, as she nervously pulled at the buckle on her jeans belt.

"Gee, Audrey, I'm gone for a few days and you get new

friends? I thought we were best friends. I thought you hated those girls as much as I did. Hillary and Cassie still make comments sometimes when they pass me in the hall. I can't hang out with them."

Audrey said pleadingly, "Gretch, they're so nice to me, and Lindsay said you could join us. Maybe they've changed. I don't think Cassie actually is in the group anymore. Give them a chance, Gretch. Do it for me? Please?"

"O.K., Audrey," replied Gretchen reluctantly. "You're my friend. I'll do it for you."

Audrey hugged her friend and promised her that she would have a good time. As they approached the hill, Jessica and Lindsay were deep in conversation, with Hillary and Brianna looking on. Jessica looked up and smiled, telling both girls she was glad they joined them. The remaining few minutes of recess were filled with comments about clothing and celebrities, and the upcoming fifth grade math test and who was planning to study with whom. Hillary made a joke about some girl's ugly outfit, and all her friends laughed. Lindsay complained that she felt fat in her skirt and blouse, and complimented Audrey on her butterfly hair clips. Audrey smiled and said little. Gretchen had nothing to say, and no one spoke to her.

Although always reluctant to leave the freedom of fresh air for the confines of work and responsibility, Audrey and her new friends were happy and animated on their walk back into the building — whispering, giggling, making plans. Of the group, only Gretchen was silent and serious. But nobody noticed.

During social studies, which finished just before lunch, Gretchen never once made eye contact with Audrey, even though Audrey tried on a number of occasions to get her attention. Map skills was boring, and when Audrey turned to roll her eyes at Gretchen, her friend looked past her and then back down at her textbook. Maybe all she needs is time, thought Audrey. Maybe things would be different at lunch.

When the class broke for lunch, Audrey tried to persuade Gretchen to join the girls at their table.

"Look, Audrey," said Gretchen angrily, "I told you I don't want to hang around with them. Nobody spoke to me out there, and I had a horrible time. Go sit with your big shot friends, if you like. I'd rather eat alone."

"Then I won't eat with them either," answered Audrey, hardly able to believe that she was in the process of throwing away an amazing social opportunity. "Let's sit together in our usual spot, O.K.?" She smiled and patted Gretchen on the shoulder.

As they settled in, they compared homemade sandwiches and talked about movie rentals. Audrey casually glanced a couple of times at Lindsay's table, wishing she could be in on their conversations. As she started to say something about Gretchen's art work, Brianna approached them from across the cafeteria. Wearing a green and blue polka dot skirt with a green ruffled hem, a matching blue top, and a green headband, Brianna looked like she'd stepped out of a fashion magazine. Audrey wondered where these girls shopped for clothes. Brianna spoke between crunches of apple.

"Come and join us, Audrey. You said you'd have lunch with us, remember?"

Audrey answered, "Gretchen and I are having lunch together, like we always do, but I'd like to eat with you, too."

Brianna smiled and returned to her friends. Shortly after, Jessica, Hillary, Lindsay and Brianna gathered up their lunches and made their way to Audrey and Gretchen's table. Both girls were nearly speechless when the group put down their plates, cups and napkins and casually arranged themselves at the table, chatting and joking.

"Well, Aud," said Jessica, "you need some fun, so here we are! Right girls?"

The others nodded in agreement and continued a conversation they were apparently having at their own table.

"I don't care about her apology, Brianna," said Jessica. "I said Cassie's out. Let her hang out with Melissa and Ashley and all those losers. See how she likes that for a while."

As Jessica opened her bag of chips, Hillary asked, "Jess, did you ever find your bracelet?"

Lindsay interjected, "It's still missing!"

"I think I can answer for myself, Lindsay, if you don't

mind!" snapped Jessica. Lindsay followed with a quick apology.

"To answer your question, Hill, no, it never turned up. But the good news is my dad is going to file a claim and get me a replacement!"

Said Brianna, "I thought your parents said they wouldn't do that."

"Well, I put on the old waterworks for my dad. You know what a softy he is. He's such a sweetie. Anyhow, my mom wasn't happy at first, but he talked her into it."

As the girls were displaying their admiration for their leader's undeniable ability to get what she wanted, Hillary said, "OMG! Take a look at what just walked in!"

All eyes turned to Alisha Krantz, who arrived late to lunch. Alisha was overweight and wore very thick glasses because of an eye problem she had had since birth.

"If I were that fat I'd crawl into a big hole and stay there!" said Lindsay in horror.

"Can you spell 'fat'?" smirked Brianna.

"Yeah, A-L-I-S-H-A," spelled Hillary in a loud sing-songy voice. Her performance was met by laughter and snickers.

"She's lucky her eyesight is so bad. At least she can't see how ugly she is!" wisecracked Jessica.

Jessica, Lindsay, Hillary, and Brianna exploded into laughter, Hillary and Brianna looking directly at Alisha. Alisha walked with her head down until she found a quiet, vacant corner.

Gretchen was remembering the nasty comments Hillary had made about her extra weight and how they'd hurt her so badly. She took this remark personally. Gathering her empty bags and papers, she left the table and sat elsewhere. Audrey stood up to follow when Jessica stopped her.

"Audrey, Gretchen is all right, but she's just the kind of friend that will hold you back. She doesn't mix well with people. She takes things too seriously. I mean, look what she was doing today. She was pulling you away from us. She's probably jealous that you have us for friends. We had to come and rescue you. And we never visit other tables. That's how much we think of you."

"And besides," added Lindsay, "she's so pudgy, and you know she'll just get fatter. They always do. And what's with the clothes? Pretty dorky."

"Yeah, Audrey," said Hillary, "you're really cool. And with just a little help from the Style Girls you will be so awesome. And we can go shopping and spend time at the club."

"You gotta get with the program, girl!" exclaimed Jessica.

Lindsay patted Audrey on the back, and she got the same warm sunshine feeling that she had felt at Jessica's house.

After lunch the girls made for their hill, and Audrey looked back once to see Gretchen walking with Alisha. Maybe her new friends were right.

CHAPTER
18

Never injure a friend, even in jest.

– *Cicero*

Through the end of April and the beginning of May, Audrey was splitting her recess and lunchroom time between her two sets of friends. However, the split was gradually becoming less and less even. She couldn't help it; Lindsay and Jessica were right. They were more fun and interesting and exciting than Gretchen. Besides, kids she didn't even know were staring at her as she passed by, like she was a celebrity or something. She was with the best group in school and now she was really somebody — she couldn't deny that it felt good. It felt GREAT!

But Audrey still wanted to be Gretchen's friend. It just frustrated her that Gretchen couldn't get with the program. How hard would it be for her to relax a little and join in, make a few jokes, and not be so touchy about things? Audrey was getting tired of trying to be everybody's pal. She wished it didn't have to be so hard. The girls were so nice to her, and Gretchen was making it so difficult. Maybe Jessica was right — that Gretchen was just jealous of Audrey's great friends and was trying to ruin it for her.

Lately, while lunching at Jessica's table, Audrey was noticing that Gretchen was eating with Alisha, and that they seemed to be enjoying each other's company. The new eating arrangement served as the perfect opportunity for Jessica and her girls to proudly reassure Audrey that she was lucky to be with them.

Audrey continued to be picked up from the after-school program by Mrs. Hart, spending a couple of hours a day at Gretchen's house until Mrs. Tabor returned from work. However, it was becoming obvious that the dynamics of the friendship were changing. While the girls were still playing board games and watching T.V., Audrey was peppering their conversations with comments about some new article of clothing she had to have or new nail polish color that was "totally in." Gretchen was displaying boredom at Audrey's newly acquired interests, and Audrey, in turn, was sighing and rolling her eyes at her friend's apparent ignorance of fashionable things. In addition, Audrey was consistently declining Gretchen's invitations to shoot hoops in her driveway — formerly a favorite pastime of both girls; Audrey was afraid that she would chip a newly manicured nail. The visits were becoming less fun for both of them.

CHAPTER

19

The only way to have a friend is to be one.

– *Ralph Waldo Emerson*

Lucy Ruggerio, a fifth grader who played violin in the school concerts, was at her coat hook rummaging through her backpack. As Audrey and Jessica headed down the hall for recess, Lucy looked up and smiled warmly at Audrey.

"Hi, Audrey, how's it going?"

"Fine, thanks, Lucy," replied Audrey brightly. "Aren't you going out for recess?"

"Yeah, but I've just gotta find a notebook first for writing, or I'm in trouble!"

"I hope you find it," replied Audrey. As she and Jessica continued down the hall, with Jessica picking up the pace, Audrey turned back to Lucy and added, "See you outside!"

"You don't have to smile at everybody who says hello, you know!" advised Jessica to Audrey, as they walked toward the big double doors.

For the past few weeks Audrey had been greeted by various students — some of whom she sort of knew and others she didn't know at all. She always acknowledged these salutations with a smile and a nod, or a friendly "hi."

"They don't expect us to really be their friends," continued Jessica. "If we smiled and talked to everybody we'd be just like the rest of them. But we have more style, we're smarter, funnier, and just better all around, and they all know it. That's why they say hello to you now. Audrey, you are COOL. Accept it, and act like it — for all of us."

As she concluded her lecture, Jessica bounced a playful hip into Audrey and, with a warm smile, added, "Am I right, girlfriend?"

Audrey, caught off guard by Jessica's playfulness, giggled, "You're right, I guess."

"You guess?" gasped Jessica in mock astonishment.

"I mean," answered Audrey, "You are absolutely right!"

"Correct-o-mundo, kiddo!"

Jessica and Audrey approached the playground door, cleaving their way easily through the gridlock of students. They were greeted at their usual spot by Brianna, Hillary, and Lindsay. Lindsay and Brianna seemed to be having a disagreement.

"Jess," pleaded Lindsay, "didn't you say we were hanging out Saturday at the mall?"

"I said we were hanging out, but I didn't mention the mall."

Brianna looked at Lindsay with a self-satisfied smile on her face.

Jessica added, "I figure we'll meet at my house and go to the square, do a little shopping — boutique stuff, have lunch, come back to my house and hang out there. You up for that, Audrey? We generally either do a Friday evening or Saturday afternoon thing, you know?" Jessica turned to the rest and added, "Bring your cash or your plastic, and we'll have some fun!"

While Audrey smiled and nodded, she wondered how anyone her age would be permitted to have a credit card. Audrey's parents had brought her up to believe that a credit card was an important but dangerous spending tool. Even her mom and dad were very careful about where and how often they themselves used their cards. Many times she listened as her parents discussed the difficulties of credit card spending and the danger of increasing credit bills that couldn't be paid. Audrey knew how long it had taken her mom and dad to work and save for the down payment on their house, and the family had been very frugal during that time with their "plastic." Even now Audrey rarely saw her mom pay for things with a card. She planned on joining the girls for the day, but, considering the small amount of allowance money she had sitting in her drawer, Audrey didn't plan on buying very much.

"There's this opal bracelet at Stevens Jewelers that is to die for, I swear!" exclaimed Jessica.

"Jessica," asked Lindsay, "didn't you just get that emerald bracelet?"

Jessica turned to Lindsay with a scowl, punctuated by a curled lip. "So what? And how is my jewelry your business, anyway, Lindsay?"

"I didn't mean anything by it. I just thought —"

"Well," interrupted Jessica, "don't think!"

At that exchange, Brianna and Hillary looked at each other and down at the grass. Lindsay looked embarrassed, shrugging and smiling sheepishly to the others. She became quiet. Audrey looked at her and began to feel uncomfortable. She decided to move the conversation on to one of Lindsay's favorite topics.

"Have you seen the bathing suits in the May issue of *Seventeen*? Oh, wow! I'll have to lose a few pounds!"

Lindsay's eyes lit up, and she answered, "Oh, just a couple of pounds, Audrey, and you will be a movie star! I think I have way too much flab, though! But by June we can both be skinny and gorgeous together. I'll show you how."

At that moment, Gretchen and Alisha appeared in their general vicinity. Alisha was eating from a bag of potato chips. Hillary saw them and jabbed Brianna saying loudly with a sly smile, "I think Audrey here doesn't want to be flubby like her friend, Gretchen."

"Flubby" was a concoction made up by Jessica, a combination of the words, "chubby" and "flabby," and quite a source of linguistic pride for the Style Girls.

Before Audrey could defend her friend, Brianna added, "Or Gretchen's fatso pal, Alisha!"

With that, Hillary, Jessica, Lindsay, and Brianna made assorted choking and gagging sounds, nearly falling to the ground in hysterical laughter. Audrey looked at her shoes and said nothing. She looked up to see Gretchen's eyes penetrating her own. At that moment the bell rang.

As the students filed into the building, Audrey, feeling sick with guilt, approached Gretchen to explain.

"Your friends are a bunch of mean stupid jerks, and so are you!" cried Gretchen, eyes red rimmed and swollen. "I never want to speak to you again, Audrey!"

Gretchen turned away abruptly and, with Alisha, disappeared in the crowd. Numbly, Audrey fell back among her new friends.

CHAPTER

20

All the wealth of the world could not buy you a friend
or pay you for the loss of one.

– C.D. Prentice

On Saturday morning, a bright and lovely spring day, Audrey's dad was dragging the lawn mower out of the shed, preparing to spend the next forty-five minutes or so "beautifying our little yard," as he liked to say. Her mom was putting the last breakfast dish in the dishwasher so that she could sit at the table and pay the weekly bills. Matthew was downstairs in the family room, still in his pajamas, watching cartoons and playing with his beloved set of trucks. His fire truck was presently involved in a daring rescue operation taking place on the second bookcase shelf. Audrey was in her room staring at the contents of her closet. (When she behaved in a similar manner at the refrigerator door, her dad would always ask if she was waiting for something to fall out at her.)

The problem was, none of her clothes seemed right

anymore. Jeans didn't look right with shirts; shoes didn't match; everything looked old, worn out, drab, not cool. She was just imagining what outfits the girls were going to show up in this morning at Jessica's house. Not to mention those little extras, like hair clips and earrings. Audrey noticed recently that Lindsay had started wearing a silver ankle bracelet with a pink heart. It set off her sandals perfectly.

When Audrey had broached the subject of earrings with her mother a week earlier, the conversation had turned angry.

"Mom, you should see how beautiful Lindsay looks. She wears everything that matches, and her hair is always perfect and so long. And when we were over at Jessica's she had these moon and star earrings. Do you think I can get my ears pierced and maybe get really nice earrings like Lindsay's?"

Audrey and her mother were returning from a quick stop at the supermarket for dinner groceries. It was six thirty, and Mrs. Tabor was exhausted from a long day at work. A serious conversation was the last thing she wanted at this particular time; however, she gathered her thoughts together, waited several seconds and began.

"First of all, honey, I understand how impressive these girls can be. They seem to have a great deal. Certainly, if Jessica's home is any indication, this is a wealthy crowd. Now that means that Lindsay, Jessica, and the rest have parents who can afford to go to fancy stores and outfit their daughters in expensive things, and lots of them. They probably have many clothing choices — several blouses that match a single pair of pants. We don't have unlimited funds, so none of us has unlimited choices. Do you understand?"

"Yes, I know," answered Audrey. "But what about just getting my ears pierced so I can wear some nice jewelry?"

"Audrey," began Mrs. Tabor slowly, "I don't know how many times you have heard my opinion on hoops and dangling earrings on children. I don't approve. Besides, those hanging things are dangerous if they catch on anything; I feel they are inappropriate for any girl under the age of fourteen."

"But that's high school!" shouted Audrey. "I have to wait till high school? That's not fair! I'll be the only girl in school without pierced ears! Everyone has pierced ears! You treat me like a baby!"

"First of all, Audrey, stop shouting at me immediately! And I hardly think that not having pierced ears makes you a baby. If you ask me, whining makes you a baby. This whole fashion thing is ridiculous. Why, when I was your age, earrings and nail polish were unheard of. Decent girls from nice families didn't use makeup or wear these other things until they were in high school. And even then, long dangling earrings were never worn in school."

Mrs. Tabor pulled into the driveway and parked the car. Before her mother opened the back door to pull the bags out, Audrey had slammed her own door and angrily made her way to the side steps.

Turning quickly, Mrs. Tabor called to Audrey. "You get right back here and help me with these bags, young lady!"

After piling the grocery bags on the kitchen table and the counter, Audrey spoke, trying not to cry. "Things aren't the same as when you were my age, Mom. You should come to school and see that almost every girl has her ears pierced. Even a few boys!"

Mrs. Tabor replied, "Don't get me started on boys wearing earrings!"

Audrey continued, "But, really, Mom, most of the girls just wear little earrings or studs. And they're really nice kids. The teachers don't mind either. I just feel so dorky. Can't I be just a little cool — with little earrings?"

Mrs. Tabor smiled slightly at Audrey's plaintive sweetness, and the confrontation ended on a hopeful note. As Audrey helped her mom empty the bags, her mom promised to give the matter some serious thought.

Last week's earring issue was one thing. This morning, Audrey had to figure out how to make her wardrobe look cool, and she had to do it soon because she was supposed to be at Jessica's by ten thirty, and it was already nine thirty.

Thirty-five minutes and one gorgeous French braid later, Audrey bounded down the stairs looking for her mother. She wore her best jeans, accompanied by a green and white shirt and a matching green hair ribbon that she found, with great surprise, in her bureau drawer.

Ten minutes later, Mrs. Tabor was backing the car out of the Morton's driveway as Audrey was making her way to Jessica's open kitchen door.

All but Hillary were already there. The girls were in the kitchen, some sitting, others standing. They were discussing the day's itinerary as Audrey walked in.

"So, we'll go downtown and hit the stores — Greenwood Gift Shoppe, Stevens's, Nelson's Boutique," directed Jessica.

Lindsay continued, "I'm totally up for an elegant lunch at The Grille."

Brianna and Jessica, nodding in agreement, looked up simultaneously and saw Audrey walk in. Brianna waved and smiled.

"Hey," cried Jessica, "Who said you could walk in without knocking, Audrey?"

"Oh, I'm sorry," apologized Audrey. Her face dropped in embarrassment.

"Hey, I'm just kidding around with you, Aud! Don't get so sensitive!" laughed Jessica. At that moment, Hillary walked in without knocking, just as Audrey had, and everyone burst into cackles of laughter.

Hillary looked a little confused, but managed a smile. Audrey smiled and laughed a little, too. She figured she'd better learn to take a joke, if she were going to fit in. She just wasn't always sure when they were joking.

"So, Aud," said Lindsay suddenly, "are you armed and

dangerous?"

The group looked expectantly at Audrey, who just stared back blankly. She had no idea what Lindsay was talking about.

"You know," explained Jessica, "did you bring your plastic? The stores are waiting!"

"No, my mother doesn't let me use a credit card, and, actually, I have only a little allowance money to spend. So, I just won't buy too much," answered Audrey. She tried to sound matter-of-fact, but inside was feeling like she wanted to cry.

The girls looked at each other. Then Jessica said reassuringly, "Don't worry about anything, Audrey. You'll have a great day!"

With that, Hillary opened the door, and the group dashed out in pursuit of a day of serious shopping.

———————————

The day was a whirlwind of excitement for Audrey. The girls loved her green-ribboned French braid. Jessica said it needed some adornment, and bought her a beautiful green and blue butterfly clip, which she placed in her hair immediately. Audrey told Lindsay that she would probably be getting her ears pierced soon.

"Well that settles it, girlfriend!" exclaimed Lindsay at Audrey's news. "We are going right this minute to the gift shop to find you an awesomely amazing pair of earrings!"

Upon sorting through the enormous variety of earrings hanging on several revolving displays, Lindsay stopped at a pair of blue flowers that dangled at the bottom of an inch and half long silver chain. Audrey fell in love with the little hanging flowers and imagined them gently dancing by her neck. And with her French braid, it would all be perfect. Her daydreams of beauty quickly returned to reality, however, when she remembered that this was exactly the type of jewelry expressly forbidden by her mom.

Audrey lovingly stroked the delicate light blue center stone surrounded by the thin silver petals, and murmured to Lindsay, "I can't buy these."

Wrapping her arm around Audrey's shoulder, Lindsay replied, "Then I'll buy them for you!" She pulled out her "plastic" — one of the gift cards she had in her purse, and slapped it down on the counter.

As the cashier dropped the little treasure into the bag, Lindsay beamed with pride and Audrey's heart was overflowing with feelings of friendship. How could she tell her friend that she wasn't allowed to wear the earrings after so gracious an offer? "Thank you, thank you," was all she could say.

Turning with Lindsay to leave the store, Audrey looked up to see Hillary glancing at them as she stood by the greeting cards. She seemed angry, but Audrey decided that it was probably just her imagination.

Lunch consisted of salads, sandwiches, and lemonade. It cost Audrey all the money she brought with her, but she couldn't let the girls pay for anything else. Brianna and Hillary got an ice cream cone, but Jessica was too full and Lindsay and Audrey were watching their weight for the fast approaching swimsuit season.

Loaded down with various cosmetics, articles of clothing, and jewelry, the girls returned to Jessica's. It was an exhausted pile of people, packages, and plastic that tumbled onto the family room sofa at approximately three o'clock that afternoon. Mr. and Mrs. Morton were preparing to go to the club for dinner, and Brianna's mother offered to take all the girls home. Lindsay stayed on.

Mrs. Dean dropped off Hillary first. Near Gretchen's street, Hillary's was a well tended, yet modest home, similar to Audrey's. And hadn't Gretchen told Audrey that Hillary lived nearby? Hillary, who used to be Gretchen's best friend?

But Audrey felt too tired to think about all that now. A few minutes later, she waved goodbye to Brianna and her mother as she approached the side entrance of her house. Opening the door, Audrey quickly slipped her new earrings into her jeans pocket and hid the empty bag.

21

There is no friend like an old friend
Who has shared our morning days
No greeting like his welcome,
No homage like his praise.

– Oliver Wendell Holmes

Throughout the month of May, Audrey was like a tulip at morning — opening to the sun, expectant with life. Her new, exciting friends liked her, and even thought she was attractive. What's more, students she hardly knew recognized her by name. She always had things to do and places to go on the weekends with the most popular kids in school. Audrey basked in the warmth of "belonging," and felt sorry for those whose lives didn't match hers. Jessica was correct — everybody wished they could be one of the Style Girls.

Since their blow-up, however, Gretchen and Audrey had terminated their after-school arrangement at Gretchen's house. This meant that, once again, Audrey wasn't getting picked up from school 'til around six o'clock. It had become not only a long, boring afternoon but an uncomfortable one

— with both girls working hard to avoid each other's company. However, the difficulty mercifully ended when Lindsay's mother approved of Lindsay's proposal to have Audrey come home with her every day after school. This meant that for the first time since kindergarten, Audrey did not have to spend time in a daycare-type program. She was very excited.

In response to the kind gesture, Mrs. Tabor called Mrs. Brentoff, and on the following Saturday morning, the two enjoyed several cups of tea and scones in the Brentoffs' kitchen. As their conversaton progressed, Audrey's mom became comfortable as she learned that Lindsay's family seemed lovely. Mrs. Brentoff was bright and gracious — very like the way Lindsay presented herself at the Tabors' dinner. She spoke proudly of her daughter's good grades and study habits, all of which Mrs. Tabor felt would be a positive influence on Audrey. And she was particularly pleased that Audrey did not have to stay late at school anymore.

However, Alice Tabor's approval of the Brentoffs did not override the shock and disappointment she had felt when Audrey had announced that she wouldn't be spending the ends of her afternoons at the Harts' anymore.

Nearly out of breath at the unexpected news, Mrs. Tabor slowly sank into the family room sofa. "Audrey, are you telling me that you and Gretchen, your best friend since leaving Boston, are not speaking to each other anymore?"

Audrey had known that this conversation would have

to happen, but she wasn't looking forward to it. Standing in the middle of the room, she replied, "Well, she was the one who said she never wanted to speak to me again, and then she walked away with her new best friend."

Mrs. Tabor shook her head slowly. "But that doesn't sound anything like the Gretchen I know. I might not have known her as long as I've known Milly, but I think I'm a good enough judge of character to recognize a sweet, caring person when I see one. Audrey, something must have happened to make Gretchen say that to you."

Shifting from one foot to the other and tugging at the pocket of her jeans, Audrey explained, "I tried to have her join Lindsay and the girls, but she didn't want to. She wouldn't even try for me. I really tried, Mom. I even left them during lunch so that Gretchen and I could eat — just the two of us. But she doesn't want me to have any other friends but her."

As a second thought Audrey added, "She even called me a stupid jerk! I've never called anybody a name that bad — not ever!"

Audrey's mother was silent for a moment, and then began deliberately, "Lindsay and Jessica seem like smart, well-mannered girls. They come from good homes and have pleasant mothers. But, Audrey, I want to make this very clear: you will never be able to have all the things their parents can buy them. And that could become a real problem for you."

Pausing briefly to further gather her thoughts, Mrs.

Tabor continued. "Audrey, something here just doesn't sound right to me. What would make Gretchen, of all people, behave so rudely toward these girls and speak so insultingly to you? Is there something you're not telling me? It would break my heart to see you and Gretchen lose each other's friendship. Remember that saying Gramma used to recite: 'Make new friends and keep the old...'"

"I know, Mom," she interrupted, "but it's not like that. I'm not calling her, and I know she'll never call me. It's over. Anyway, my new friends are really nice, and we have a great time together, and they're the most popular kids in school. I'm really happy, Mom."

The conversation ended. Audrey was relieved it was over, but her mother was feeling that the matter was not resolved. She decided, however, to leave things alone and let the situation develop on its own. But as Audrey started up the stairs, Mrs. Tabor suddenly remembered something, and called her name. Midway up the staircase, Audrey turned around.

"Audrey, did you ever call Milly back? It's been quite a while."

She answered quietly, "Oh, I guess I forgot."

"Well," said Mrs. Tabor, in a voice as quiet as Audrey's, "then I guess you forgot Milly's tenth birthday, too. It was the day you spent shopping with your friends."

CHAPTER

22

Whether our dwelling be a castle or a cabin,
our trials will be lighter and our comforts will be richer
if we have a true friend.

– Thain Davidson

Audrey felt badly about forgetting to call Milly and missing her birthday. She kept making mental notes to herself to give her a call and try to get their friendship back on track, but every time she began thinking about it, her new busy social life would distract her. Hillary would call with a funny story, or Jessica would invite her out to a movie. Of course, Lindsay had become her after school pal. Audrey began thinking of Milly less and less, and then finally not at all.

The Brentoffs' house soon became a comfortable second home to Audrey. Every day after school, the girls would run to the family room, throwing their backpacks to the floor while diving into the plush emerald green sofas. Shoes were kicked off while Mrs. Brentoff brought them tall, delicious iced teas with fresh lime. Sometimes, if she had spent the morning in the kitchen, Mrs. Brentoff would also bring a plate of newly baked chocolate chip cookies. Most other days, she was busy in some other part of the house, leaving the girls to find their own snacks.

About three weeks into their new arrangement, Lindsay surprised Audrey one day by demonstrating her own talent in the kitchen.

"This mocha cake is absolutely to die for!" boasted Lindsay, as she was assembling all kinds of ingredients and measuring tools on the counter. "No one can make this cake and frosting the way I do. Everyone says it's better than from a bakery. Wait 'til you taste it, Audrey. You won't believe it!"

Audrey was already impressed just by the volume of stuff lying all over the counter — flour, cocoa, coffee, eggs…

"You mean you can make a cake from scratch? The closest I ever came once to baking anything was when I sliced those ready-made cookie things you get in the store refrigerator. I think I burned a couple."

Lindsay spoke as she read her recipe card. "There are lots of things I can make. Watching my mom since I was a little kid got me interested. My mom says that maybe someday I'll be a famous chef or something, or maybe a person who plans big parties for celebrities!" As she measured the salt, she said, "Hey, Aud, hand me that vanilla."

After Lindsay beat the batter into a shiny, silky medium brown cream, she separated it evenly into two separate layer pans. While she slipped the pans into the preheated oven, she said, "Oh, Audrey, would you mind clearing up the counter while I run upstairs to tell my mom something? I'll be right back."

Ten minutes later Lindsay returned to find Audrey wiping down the cleaned counters. Most of the bowls, spoons and cups were sitting spotlessly in the drainer.

"Oh, Audrey, you didn't have to do all this! Really, thank you so much. I didn't mean to be gone so long."

Audrey beamed, feeling proud that she could be of obvious assistance to her friend, who seemed never to need any help from anybody.

"Oh, that's O.K. You worked hard at making the cake. I didn't mind helping you clean. Are you going to frost the cake, too?"

"Audrey, you're not going to believe this frosting. It's the best!" answered Lindsay, as she began to pull out the next round of ingredients.

Lindsay continued in a confidential tone, "I brought this cake to the Christmas party at our club. Of course, everyone loved it. And Wendy Blake — you know Wendy. She's kind of ugly with that space between her teeth and that stringy hair. She can't do anything with that hair! Well, anyway, she and her family were guests at the party that day. Frankly, I can't imagine why anyone would invite them. So, anyway, Wendy asks me for the recipe. The recipe! I mean, can you imagine?!"

At this Lindsay rolled her eyes and chortled.

Audrey smiled brightly, but couldn't quite grasp the humor. She assumed that, as usual, she was missing something.

Audrey replied, "So, you mean you wouldn't give Wendy the recipe?"

Lindsay gave a sly grin and said, "Well, after she asked me for about the *third time*, I gave her the recipe. Except I just sort of accidentally left out an ingredient or two."

As she spoke, she placed little air quotes around the word "accidentally."

"I don't share anything with losers — especially my recipes. I just wish I could have been in the room when her cake didn't come out quite right!" Lindsay giggled and bumped hips with Audrey. "But don't worry, Audrey," promised Lindsay, "you can have the full recipe any time you want it!"

Audrey responded with a wide, forced smile.

Later, Audrey had to admit that for all Lindsay's bragging, it was just about the best dessert she ever ate. She devoured two slices with a glass of milk, and wished she could have a third, but had better sense than to ask. Lindsay ate one small piece, reminding her friend that bathing suit season was fast approaching and they needed to keep their wits about them if they didn't want to look like Alisha Krantz.

For the next hour and a half, until Mrs. Tabor came, the girls thumbed through magazines, ogling clothes and hairdos. Lindsay gossiped to Audrey about the girls in school. She discussed her very strict "Loser Category": the wrong clothing or hair, too much weight, or a "bad personality" could put you right into it.

"Trust me, Aud," advised Lindsay, "you don't want to be a loser, and you don't want to be friendly with losers. That means no sharing recipes, ideas, or homework. And no big friendly, smiley 'hello's' in the hallway. Just stick with us. We'll take care of you. And, most important, always be on the lookout for some real good gossip! We always share!"

That evening while Audrey worked on her homework in long division, she became distracted from time to time, thinking about her new best friends. So many rules to remember and new ways to behave. So demanding was this world of popularity.

CHAPTER
23

My best friend is the one who brings out the best in me.

– Henry Ford

The Saturdays spent shooting baskets and watching videos and popping corn with Gretchen were now replaced with shopping sprees, luncheon dates, and gossiping. Sometimes Audrey would spend time with only Lindsay, sometimes with only Hillary, other times with Jessica, Lindsay, and the rest. The girls were always buying things for Audrey. Sometimes a bracelet or nail polish from the Card & Gift Shoppe, or a cute T-shirt that one of the group decided she "absolutely had to have." After Audrey had gotten her ears pierced, as her mother had finally promised, Lindsay and Jessica were working overtime in choosing just the right earrings for their new friend. Of the earrings they bought her, there wasn't a single style that Audrey's mom would ever let her wear. Still, Audrey beamed with gratitude as she carried her bags of gifts.

Audrey didn't really mind all the errands that the girls would send her on or the extra chores they had her do, like throwing their lunch trash away in the "caf" or washing dishes at someone's house. She figured it was little enough payment for all the things they continued to buy her. After all, if she was going to be one of the Style Girls, she had to look like one. She just *had* to look like one of them. But how to explain her suddenly expanding wardrobe to her mother was a problem that was beginning to gnaw at Audrey's stomach. She knew she couldn't just appear at the breakfast table morning after morning dressed in new clothes. Her mother would never approve of the girls buying Audrey clothes. She'd probably make her take them back to the store. That would be so embarrassing. The girls would make fun of her. So, the new things went to the back of her closet.

After giving the matter some thought, Audrey decided that she could stuff a new outfit in her backpack and change after she got to school. She could even take along those great new earrings. It could work, because she could change back into her old clothes before her mom picked her up at Lindsay's. She would have to explain it to Lindsay and get her to promise not to say a word to anyone, but she knew that Lindsay would understand, because they had become such good friends.

On one Saturday in early June, Hillary's mom took Hillary and Audrey to the mall. While Mrs. Wright was having her hair done, the girls browsed through the stores. In one department store, Hillary spied a pink and black polka dot mini skirt with matching cropped top, and couldn't take her eyes off the outfit. Grabbing Audrey by the arm, with eyes flashing, she exclaimed, "Audrey, you and I should dress the same in these clothes! We should come to school dressed alike. It would be so cool!"

Audrey loved the skirt and matching top and was beginning to imagine herself in it. She had a vision of everyone in school just drooling over how great she looked. And even more than that — it would make everyone see how much a part of the most popular group she had become. But then she looked at the price tag and her vision quickly faded.

"Oh, Hillary, this is way too expensive. I can't buy it, and you can't pay for one of these either, let alone two!"

"Are you kidding? Audrey, what planet do you live on? This is nothing compared to other things my mom has bought me. And besides, my mom says that it's really important to dress well, and if I see something really cool I can use this card that she gave me." As she said this, she pulled a shiny gold-colored gift card out of her shoulder bag and waived it in Audrey's face.

"Well," murmured Audrey, "I still wouldn't feel right about it. You guys have already bought so many nice things for me."

"Yeah, and by the way, why haven't we seen you wearing any of them?"

Audrey swallowed in embarrassment, and replied, "I promise I'll be wearing them real soon."

"Well, girlfriend, add this to the list." Hillary stopped suddenly and said to Audrey. "Unless you don't *want* to dress like me. If I were Lindsay, I bet you'd say yes right away. Do you like Lindsay better than me? Is that it?"

"Of course not, Hillary! I would love to dress like you," Audrey assured her friend.

"That settles it, then. Let's try these on. If they fit, we'll be twins at school on Monday, O.K.?" Hillary wrapped her arm around Audrey's shoulder.

For the next twenty minutes, Hillary led Audrey from counter to counter, finding matching black headbands and pink earrings. Pink sandals from the shoe store three doors down were even thrown into the mix.

"You know, Aud," said Hillary as they looked at the summer bag display, "I'm glad we're going to wear these cool dresses. I'm sick of Lindsay always thinking that she has the best taste and the coolest things. Aren't you sick of all her bragging?"

Audrey was looking inside a large pastel striped straw tote bag, wishing she had one like it. "I guess she does brag sometimes, but she's great. I really like her."

"Oh, hey, I love Lindsay. We've been friends for a long time. But, you know. I mean, you're at her house every day. She must drive you a little crazy sometimes, right?"

Audrey was feeling very close and special with Hillary at

that moment. She felt as though Hillary wanted her confidence, and Audrey wanted to confide just to prove that she could be a good and interesting friend. So often she didn't feel very interesting at all among such a sophisticated group of girls.

"Well, Lindsay brags a lot about her baking. But it is really delicious, though."

"Don't tell me," said Hillary, "she made you her mocha cake that is the best in the world." She said "best in the world" in a mocking, sing-songy voice.

"Well, yes. She does kind of brag."

"*Kind* of brag? Are you kidding? Her baking is the best; her nail polish is the best; her clothes. It's endless. And she's always tossing her hair around like it's made of gold or something. My mother told me never to brag about myself. It's bad form."

"My mother taught me the same thing. She says it's obnoxious," agreed Audrey readily.

Walking out of the store, arms linked, Audrey was feeling like she was truly bonding with Hillary. She felt as though they were twins in spirit as well as dress. She was also beginning to feel comfortable about being dressed by her girlfriends.

As they headed back to where Mrs. Wright was having her hair done, store bags in hand, Audrey was carefully going over in her mind how she would slip the store bag past her mom and furthermore, how she would hide her new clothes as she left for school Monday morning.

CHAPTER

24

We should ask from friends and do for friends

only what is good.

– Cicero

Throughout that weekend, Audrey worried about the new clothes. On Sunday night, she slept fitfully and dreamed erratically. Some dreams were filled with polka dots, friends, and admirers. But twice, these pleasant scenes turned to nightmares, where she found herself standing shoeless in the school hall wearing old torn clothes, being ridiculed by her schoolmates and reprimanded by her angry mother. The ordeal came to an end when Audrey awoke the next morning at six, a full hour before her alarm was set to ring.

Tired and with a slight ache in her stomach, Audrey quickly pulled her store bags out from the back of her closet. Everything — skirt and top, sandals, headband, and earrings — was neatly placed in her backpack, and all was cleverly concealed by her math textbook, spiral notebook, and other school tools. With that completed, Audrey dressed herself in her usual school attire — jeans, T-shirt, sneakers, and socks. It was now six thirty, and she was ready for breakfast a full hour earlier than usual. She decided to sit in her rocking chair and read her independent reading book, the first in a series of four. If she finished it today, she could begin reading the second book.

By seven o'clock, Audrey was losing her concentration, and the rest of the household was making its usual morning sounds. Mattie was making "vroom" noises with his trucks, water was whooshing through humming pipes, and spoons, cups and closing cabinets were offering their usual kitchen symphony. It was time for Audrey to join the Tabor Wake-up Band.

"Audrey, you startled me!" exclaimed Mrs. Tabor, as she was putting away the dishes that had been drying in the drainer. "You're up so early! Are you all right?"

"I'm fine, Mom," smiled Audrey. "I couldn't go back to sleep. The sun was shining so much through my window that I decided to get up and get ready for school."

Mrs. Tabor placed a box of blueberries on the counter. As she left the kitchen to get Matthew dressed for school she reminded Audrey to fix herself a bowl of cereal and a glass of orange juice. Audrey did as she was told, but barely ate a thing.

Twenty minutes later, Audrey was joined at the breakfast table by her brother's messy Rice Chex and her father's coffee and newspaper. Her mother was at the bathroom mirror, putting the finishing touches on her makeup while chewing the last morsel of toast and jam.

Several minutes later, Mr. Tabor quickly glanced at the clock, threw down his almost empty coffee cup and partly folded paper, told everyone to have a super day, and left the house. As his car pulled out of the driveway, Mrs. Tabor removed Matthew's bowl of soggy cereal and wiped the blob of milk from the tip of his nose. (She was about to ask how it got there, but looked at her watch and changed her mind.) Hurriedly replacing Mattie's left sneaker, and without looking up, Mrs. Tabor told Audrey to brush her teeth and make sure her backpack was in order.

Leaving for the bus, Audrey came to the conclusion that with everyone running in so many directions, she could have worn her whole new outfit — from sandals to earrings — and no one would have noticed. As a matter of fact, she figured she could have eaten a breakfast of spaghetti and meatballs wearing a prom gown and tiara, and nobody would have blinked!

As Audrey entered the building with her classmates, she made a mad dash for the girls' room, hoping that she wasn't noticed by any of her friends. She didn't want them to know that she had had to sneak the clothes out of the house. It would be too embarrassing to explain. Several frantic minutes later, old clothes stuffed into her backpack, Audrey quickly transformed herself from "Miss Nobody" into "Miss Style Girl." The person she saw in the mirror was somebody she never thought she would be. Staring back at her was a girl with long pink earrings and long, pretty auburn hair smoothly accented by a black headband. The mirror allowed her to view only part of her very short skirt, but what she saw looked totally cool. And the pink sandals made it all perfect. When Audrey walked out of the bathroom, she walked with a long, self-assured stride, a cool-girl walk that she had never had before.

Audrey searched all over for Hillary, even in Hillary's classroom, but she was impossible to locate, leaving Audrey disappointed as she entered her own classroom for the morning routine. Now she would have to wait until first recess to meet up with her "twin sister" — and she couldn't wait for everyone to see them.

Several sets of eyes followed Audrey as she approached her desk. Sophie Jackson turned around to compliment her on her outfit; Alison Kominski said she liked her earrings; three more girls asked her where she got her shoes. Audrey tried to be nonchalant about all the attention, remembering what her friends advised her about not getting overly friendly.

But amidst all the praise and admiration, there was Gretchen. When Gretchen passed Audrey's desk she looked at her in a strange way — almost as if she were disgusted. Jessica had said a few times that Gretchen was just jealous, and she was probably right. Audrey decided to ignore her. But it made her feel sad, even though she barely allowed herself to admit it.

After the longest morning that Audrey could remember and a math lesson that went by in a forgettable blur, it was finally time for first recess. As students found their classroom friends or waited in the hall for friends from other rooms, Audrey caught up with Lindsay. Lindsay was also dressed particularly well on this day in a green and blue tie-dyed skirt and top. Her ponytail was set off by a small blue scarf. She wore blue sandals and matching earrings and bracelet. Her nail polish was pale peach. She was gorgeous.

"Lindsay, you look amazing today!" said Audrey.

"Oh, thanks, Aud," she answered, smoothing down a skirt that needed no smoothing and straightening a ponytail that needed no straightening. "That is a pretty nice skirt and top you're wearing, too. It must be new. I've never seen you wear it before."

Audrey wanted to tell her about her arrangement with Hillary, but decided to surprise her when they got outside. She couldn't wait to see everyone's face when she and Hillary stood together. It would be so much fun to have a twin for the day. They would be like celebrities on their schoolyard hill.

As Lindsay and Audrey left the building and walked toward their spot, the little figure of pink with black polka dots got closer and closer. When finally they all met, Hillary and Audrey hugged and Jessica and Brianna giggled. But Lindsay froze, as still and stiff as a branch on a windless day. The color drained from her face as it lost all expression. She stared at Hillary, lips becoming thinner and eyes narrowing. The rest of the group stopped in silence.

"I don't understand, Hillary," began Lindsay. "You and I bought this skirt and everything else last week and made a promise to wear them together today. I even marked it on my calendar."

Audrey couldn't believe that this was happening. Today was supposed to be such a good day.

Hillary looked directly at Lindsay with wide innocent eyes and replied sweetly, "I have no idea what you're talking about. Audrey and I made these plans a long time ago, didn't we, Aud?"

Audrey knew that this statement was not true. They had made their plans only two days before. But if she corrected Hillary she would make her look like a liar. Was it possible that Hillary forgot her plans with Lindsay?

Hillary continued calmly, "I know we bought our clothes together, but we never said exactly when we were going dress alike. You obviously misunderstood me, Lindsay. I'm sorry if I wasn't clear."

"I don't misunderstand anybody, Hillary. But, don't worry. I'll never make plans with you again." Lindsay turned to Audrey and said, "Audrey, did you and Hillary really promise to dress alike a long time ago?"

Hillary and the others looked expectantly at Audrey, who swallowed hard and answered, "Yeah, we actually did. I'm really sorry, Lindsay. I didn't know." Afterwards she could have sworn she saw a sly upturn to Hillary's mouth.

Lindsay forgave Audrey and assured her that none of it was her fault, but she refused to speak with Hillary for the rest of the day. Jessica and Brianna changed the subject, opening discussion up to summer vacation schedules and country club tans.

The morning that Audrey had so looked forward to and had lost so much sleep over fell to pieces. Furthermore, instead of feeling special, she felt ugly because she had lied to so many people — even her new best buddy.

A disappointing recess over, Audrey slouched toward her classroom. Passing by the nurse's office, she thought she saw Gretchen sitting on the blue vinyl couch, and it looked like there were adults there, too. She stopped abruptly and turned back to see if the girl she had glimpsed was actually Gretchen. But as she approached the office, Nurse Daley quietly shut the door. A few minutes later, as Audrey took her classroom seat, she glanced across the room to find Gretchen's chair empty.

An unusually subdued Mrs. Antonelli asked the class to take out their social studies books.

CHAPTER
25

I cherish my friends,

for I know that of all things granted us…

none is greater than friendship.

– Pietro Aretino

The girls finished out the school year with their usual observations and judgements of others. Basically, the student population was broken down into groups labeled "idiots" if they suffered academic difficulties, "losers" if they dressed badly and had few friends, and "creeps" if they were deemed unattractive. Criteria for unattractiveness consisted of too much weight, thick glasses, and various bodily imperfections. Over the course of the final few weeks of school, Audrey had evolved into an acceptable Style Girl. When cutting remarks brought laughter, Audrey laughed too. Audrey learned how to make mean comments seem smart and witty. And she became adept at talking endlessly about clothing, diets, and other people's business. On the subject of diets, Audrey and Lindsay were nearly obsessed. Calories were counted, certain foods were eliminated, and fashion models were admired for their lack of body fat — particularly in bathing suits.

Jessica and Lindsay's training had proven effective. Because Audrey stopped smiling and talking to those not in the group, no one attempted anymore to smile and talk to her. At first she felt badly, until Jessica congratulated her for separating herself from a school full of idiots, losers and creeps. She assured Audrey that the angry looks she might receive were just based on jealousy. Because everyone wanted to be cool, beautiful, and popular.

Since the clothing incident, Lindsay had remained slightly suspicious of Hillary. Although the two began socializing again, their friendship lost its closeness. That, together with the time Audrey was spending with Lindsay every day, produced in Hillary a quiet but deep and growing resentment for Audrey.

Audrey was perfectly willing to disregard most of the student population in return for acceptance in the group. She wasn't, however, as willing to disregard Gretchen, even though it had become painfully clear that Gretchen didn't want anything to do with her. Sometimes during luncheon discussions, Audrey would glance over at Gretchen's table and watch as she and Alisha Krantz were involved in some serious talk one moment and then laughing at some funny incident the next. It made her feel bad. She told herself that with her cool friends there was no reason to be missing dorky old Gretchen.

But she missed her just the same. When approaching her in the school hallways, Audrey wanted to smile and say hello, but Gretchen always looked away. And Audrey was too proud to call out to her. She felt almost relieved that Gretchen had been absent so much lately — at least once or twice a week, it seemed.

One mid-June afternoon, the luncheon conversation turned to the subject of Gretchen, who was absent again.

"It's hard to believe that you used to hang out with Gretchen Hart," Jessica remarked to Audrey while squirting ketchup on her hotdog.

"Yeah," added Hillary. "Chubby, Flubby with all the personality of my desk chair."

The girls laughed heartily. Audrey spoke in defense of her friend.

"Gretchen is a really nice person."

"Yeah, yeah," answered Lindsay. "We've heard this all before. You're like a broken record, Audrey."

Audrey continued. "You know, Gretchen may be overweight and not wear the most cool clothes and stuff, but she's fun."

At that Hillary rolled her eyes.

"And, she can do something none of us can do," said Audrey, pausing. "She can draw so well that her pictures look good enough to enter into Greenwood High art shows."

Audrey looked at her friends to see if they were impressed.

"What does she draw?" asked Jessica.

"Pictures of girls sitting, or looking out the window and thinking."

"Wow, sounds about as exciting as her own life!" joked Lindsay.

"I guess," added Hillary, "people who have nothing to do sit around and draw. I say, 'loser.'"

"No," Audrey protested. "Really, I mean her stuff is beautiful. You can almost feel what the people in her pictures are feeling. Someday her drawings could be hanging in museums. They're really that good."

Audrey looked from face to face, and realized that no one was really paying attention. Jessica was chewing blankly on her last few potato chips; Lindsay was re-tying the scarf in her ponytail; and Hillary and Brianna were laughing together quietly. Were they laughing at Audrey's defense of Gretchen or just at some private joke? Either way, they didn't much care…

"Come on, Audrey," cried Lindsay. "Get with the program and forget about all this. Are you on for Saturday?"

Earlier in the week, Jessica had invited her friends to her club for Saturday. If the weather proved to be as warm as predicted, they would even spend time in the pool. Audrey had a new blue two-piece bathing suit acquired during a recent outing with Lindsay. They would all meet at Jessica's house and Mrs. Morton would drive them to the club in her SUV.

Audrey forgot the disagreement about Gretchen, and joined the others in an enthusiastic "yes" to Lindsay's question. How could she argue with people who were so kind to her, including her in so many fun things? She'd never been to a country club before and could barely imagine what it must be like.

CHAPTER

26

To be true friends,
you must be sure of one another.

– Leo Tolstoy

It was even more beautiful than she had imagined. The long entrance drive beyond the gate, set behind trees, was hidden from passersby, hidden from anyone not lucky enough to gain entrance. Lining the winding road were flowering trees, perfectly shaped shrubs, and flowers of many varieties in every color of the rainbow. Just the kind of flowers, thought Audrey, that she would like to have in a garden. Some yards away was a small crew of men tending the landscape, some watering, some cutting and weeding. As Mrs. Morton drove on, Audrey looked to her left and saw an impossibly perfect carpet of green that she realized was the golf course. Jessica and Lindsay had mentioned that their fathers played golf together regularly. Audrey thought of her own dad, and how he spent his leisure time on Saturdays mowing their lawn and doing odd repair jobs around the house. He was either working at his office or fixing things at home. Who had time to just golf all day or the money to pay for it? Boy, she thought, what would Milly think of all this? The thought stopped her. It was the first time in quite a while she thought of her old best friend back on Walker Avenue. At that moment, the Hitchcocks' second floor apartment suddenly appeared in her mind, with Milly's mom in the kitchen and her little sister running around making noise. She remembered the day the girls, sitting on Milly's bed, exchanged Christmas presents. Audrey began absentmindedly scratching a small rash that had recently developed on her right arm and promised herself that she would get in touch with Milly as soon as she had the time.

The memory and the promise disappeared when Audrey beheld the splendid sight before her — a large white building with four pillars and a veranda surrounded by more flowers and shrubs, all set off by a long brick walk. As Mrs. Morton drove the car around to the back, the most sparklingly clear, blue water on the planet welcomed Audrey and her friends. Beach chairs, orange and pink striped umbrellas, girls and theirs mothers being served tall drinks with straws…Audrey couldn't wait for her day at the club to begin.

As the girls took off the shorts and the tops that covered their bathing suits, Audrey couldn't help but notice that Lindsay was looking thinner than she'd ever seen her. Had she lost too much weight, or had Audrey never really paid much attention to Lindsay's actual size? She wasn't sure. She was hoping that she didn't look too fat herself in the new suit that Lindsay had bought her during one of their shopping sprees.

"Oh my God, Linds, you look so amazing in that bathing suit!" exclaimed Hillary.

"Yeah," Brianna agreed, "just like a model. I'm so jealous! Just look at my fat!" Brianna said this as she pinched the skin on her slender hips.

Audrey was looking but couldn't find the unslightly fat that Brianna was complaining about. She was beginning to feel self-conscious about the size and shape of her own body, and slouched a little as she found a chaise lounge to slide into. She had tried to follow Lindsay's dieting advice, but sometimes she really, really wanted a second helping of her mom's rosemary grilled chicken, or an extra slice of the fresh bread her mom picked up from the Italian bakery on her way home from work. She definitely was eating way less ice cream, but how could a person not eat ice cream anymore, at all, forever?

Jessica slowly removed her covering to reveal a bright pink one-piece bathing suit with an orange polka dot ruffle stitched across the top and over the left strap. It was stunning and she looked gorgeous. Slowly lowering herself into her lounge chair, she crossed her ankles, looked up at the sky, and stretched. She looked the way Audrey wanted to look. Audrey slouched a little more and threw a magazine across her lap, hoping to hide the extra fat that she hadn't worked hard enough to get rid of.

Jessica spoke. "I don't know what you're talking about. You all look great. You oughta be more like Audrey. You don't hear her whining and complaining about the way she looks in her bathing suit, do you? It doesn't seem to bother her that she's got a couple of extra pounds or that her thighs touch. I don't hear her being a big baby about wanting to look like a model. Isn't that right, Audrey?" Jessica smiled sweetly.

Audrey was mortified. Did Jessica just call her chubby? Was she complimenting her for being mature, or insulting her for being overweight? It also didn't help that the comment made Brianna snicker.

"Well, I guess I should be more careful about those second helpings," grinned Audrey sheepishly.

"Second helpings?" exclaimed Lindsay. "Haven't I told you *NO SECOND HELPINGS*? After all the time we've spent together and all the advice I've given you. Gee, Audrey, get with the program, will you?" At that, Lindsay pinned up her hair and began applying sunscreen.

"I'm dying of thirst!" said Hillary.

"Me, too," said Brianna. "How about you, Jess?"

"If I don't get something cold soon I might drink the pool water!" joked Jessica. Everyone chuckled.

No one seemed interested in Audrey's thirst — or maybe she was just still feeling hurt and was being too sensitive.

"I think we all need iced tea or lemonade or something,"

said Jessica. "What do you think, girls?" All nodded and murmured in agreement.

"I haven't seen a waitress around in I don't know how long," complained Hillary, turning in her chair to find a club employee. "Whatever they pay these people, they're not worth it. I'd give anything for a raspberry iced tea about now."

Jessica turned sweetly to Audrey and said, "Aud, would you be the best girlfriend in the world and either find a waitress, or, maybe order our drinks yourself at the bar inside? If you did that, you would totally save our lives."

Audrey took everyone's order: one raspberry iced tea, one pink lemonade, two Diet Cokes, and a root beer for herself. She wrote the information down on a piece of paper from her bag.

As she turned to go, Jessica added, "Tell them to put it on my family's tab. Oh, and Audrey, bring out some popcorn for us, O.K.? No butter."

She heard a lot of laughing and whispering from the group as she left the pool area. She told herself not to be so sensitive. They were most likely laughing at something or somebody else. She was sure of it.

Ten minutes later Audrey returned, carefully balancing a tray filled with five tall drinks, straws, napkins, and a big bowl of popcorn. The girls moved to a large round table with a striped umbrella and slid into the matching cushioned chairs.

As Audrey began to set down the tray of drinks, she tripped over the leg of Hillary's chair. Everyone gasped as she managed to save all but the lemonade, which spilled over the tray and onto the concrete. The glass, thankfully, did not fall out of the tray.

"Hey, thanks a lot, butterfingers," said Brianna. "That was mine, and I was really thirsty!"

"It's just a good thing you didn't get it on my new bathing suit," said Hillary, who sat closest to the spill. "It cost my mother a fortune at Dana's Boutique."

"Oh, for heaven's sake! Lemonade washes out! It'll probably wash right out in the pool, Hillary!" answered Jessica. "And who cares how much your bathing suit cost? People who brag about the price of things can't really afford them, right, girls?" Hillary's mouth snapped shut and she looked like a turtle in its shell. Jessica turned to Audrey and said, "Sometimes my girls have no manners. Do Brianna a real fave, Audrey, and get another one, will you? We'll owe you a big one later, won't we girls?"

Hillary stared glumly across the pool. The rest of the girls nodded and mumbled their agreement as they sipped on their drinks and reached for the popcorn.

"This is NOT unbuttered, Audrey! Maybe you eat it, but the rest of us don't put greasy, gross butter in our popcorn!" reprimanded Lindsay.

Audrey scratched her right arm and apologized. "I'm

sorry, guys. I know I said 'no butter'. Maybe the guy didn't hear me."

Said Hillary as she handed Audrey the bowl, "Be a good gofer and exchange this for something that won't make us look like Alisha Krantz." The remark got a howl from the table. Audrey laughed along, too.

After drinks and popcorn, the girls settled into their usual chatter about fashion, weight, and other people. By noon, the sun was hot, and Jessica suddenly got up, jumped into the pool, and declared the water to be cool and refreshing. One by one the others followed until all five girls were pushing and splashing in summertime heaven. While Audrey threw the beach ball back to Lindsay she couldn't help thinking that back in Boston about now she would be searching for a place to cool off — maybe a movie with a friend, or a long visit to the air-conditioned library. This was way better. This was amazing!

Marco Polo and a few other silly water games were followed by lunch, which consisted of various salads. Audrey had had her heart set on a cheeseburger with fries, but after the previous remarks about her shape, and then the buttered popcorn incident, she decided it would be best to go along with the salad. She couldn't help stealing some glances at her thighs.

Mrs. Morton, involved in an all-day tennis tournament, checked in with Jessica and the girls from time to time. Finally, at about four o'clock, she returned to tell them it was time to call it a day, which was fine with everyone. Conversations had become slower and less interesting as fatigue set in. It had been a long, active day — one of many to come — and the water and sun just about put everyone to sleep.

CHAPTER
27

True friendship is entirely unselfish;
it loves not for what it may receive,
but for what it may give.

– *J.R. Miller*

The days in July began to move along, as all summer days do. At least three days of each week consisted of group outings to the club. Audrey thought it was funny how a person can get used to anything. She barely paid attention anymore to the flower-lined drive that led to the main building. Sitting and swimming in the sun all morning and afternoon became an accepted routine. She even began to take for granted that most of her needs were being regularly met by the club staff — that is, when Audrey herself wasn't being enlisted to run errands for the girls. These errands (or "faves," as Jessica put it) took the form of message running to family members or friends, or the ordering of food or drink when a waitress couldn't be located immediately. From time to time, Audrey might fetch a sandal or some other personal article that would accidentally fall into the pool. Sometimes, when she felt angry about being the gofer, she reminded herself that Jessica and Lindsay picked her as their friend and were nice enough to include her as a summer guest. And they did, after all, buy her cool things, so she could look as nice as they did. And they always smiled at her and appreciated all the errands she ran for them.

One day as Audrey was on her way to the dining room to pick up an extra tray of fruit for her friends, Jessica caught up with her and began to walk along.

"Hey, Aud, hold on! I figured I'd keep you company for a change," said Jessica with her sweetest smile.

Audrey was startled. She hadn't expected anything like this from Jessica. But when she turned to look at her, she saw Jessica's smile, and Audrey beamed with joy and pride.

"So, girlfriend," began Jessica, "having a pretty good summer?"

"Jessica, I'm having the best summer of my life! I feel bad for anyone who has to be in some hot place with nothing fun to do. I mean, this pool is fantastic. And food is great, and —"
"Yeah, it's great," interrupted Jessica, as they approached the fruit table. Nibbling cautiously on a chocolate dipped strawberry, Jessica continued, "Listen, Aud, I wanted to ask you a question, but you have to promise not to mention this to anyone — and I mean *ANYONE*, O.K.?"

Audrey could hardly believe that the great Jessica Morton was about to confide her deepest personal feelings to her, plain old Audrey Tabor.

"Absolutely, Jess. You know you can always count on me." Audrey stood by the table in rapt attention, waiting for Jessica's nugget of vital information (a request for help? a deep dark secret?).

"I just wanted to know if Hillary ever said anything bad about me."

"Huh? Not ever. I've never heard Hillary say a single bad thing about you. Why?"

"What about Lindsay? Has Hillary ever made a bad remark about her?" Leaning closer to Audrey in a conspiring, yet threatening way, she said, "You'd tell me, wouldn't you, Audrey, if you knew about something that Hillary might have said or done against Lindsay or me?"

Audrey wondered what exactly Jessica suspected or had already figured out. She was remembering Hillary's questions about Lindsay and the conversation they had about Lindsay bragging a lot. She also remembered that she had said some things about Lindsay in response to Hillary's questions. She began to feel uncomfortable.

"Well ..." Audrey began.

"I knew it! That witch did say something! Come on, Aud. You know I'm your friend and you can trust me. And after all the time you spend with Lindsay waiting for your mom after school. You owe her."

Scratching her arm — now a deep spreading rash —

Audrey slowly answered. "Well, one day when we were out shopping around, Hillary asked me if Lindsay's bragging drives me crazy. I told her I really like Lindsay a lot. But, yeah, I guess sometimes she can brag a little. I guess Hillary has a thing about Lindsay bragging, and maybe she tells the same stories to everyone, because Hillary even mentioned Lindsay's famous mocha cake."

Jessica looked a little quizzical. Audrey paused, and then confessed to her that Lindsay had bragged about sharing her secret recipe with Wendy, but changing it to make sure it wouldn't work.

"I don't know," she said, looking down and rubbing her arm. "I guess I didn't think anything of it at the time."

"And another thing. What really happened that day when you guys showed up in the same outfit?" quizzed Jessica insistently.

"What do you mean?" Audrey was wishing she could just pick up the tray of fruit and return to the pool. She had a feeling she knew where this was leading.

"Lindsay said that she and Hillary had made plans to wear the same outfits, and on that very day, you and Hillary show up together in some other matching thing. Hillary said that you two had made plans a long time before, and you agreed. Lindsay and I think that Hillary is a liar. Did she make you lie with her, Audrey? We know it's not your fault if you did. We wouldn't be mad at you. Hillary does stuff like this a lot.

You'd be the absolute best girlfriend ever on the planet if you tell the truth."

Jessica punctuated her promise with a little nudge at Audrey's hips and a friendly arm around her shoulder.

Audrey knew that Hillary was guilty of lying that day and of wanting to gossip about Lindsay's bragging the day before. She also knew that she was wrong to have allowed herself to be pulled into Hillary's schemes. Here was Audrey's chance to make it right and explain what really happened. She knew she could trust Jessica, and that Lindsay would understand. After all, it was clearly Hillary's fault.

"You know, in a way, I'm kind of glad you asked me about this, because I was feeling really bad. Yeah, Hillary was looking to say some mean things about Lindsay. She even said she was sick of Lindsay thinking that everything she has is the best, and that it's bad manners."

"What about the dress?" pressed Jessica.

"Honest, Jessica, I never knew a single thing about her plans with Lindsay to dress the same. But when she said in front of everyone that we had made plans a long time before, I went along, because I didn't want to cause any trouble. Really. I'm sorry if I hurt anyone. I was trying *not* to. I felt bad for Lindsay when I saw how disappointed she was. But it really wasn't my fault." Audrey was close to tears, but worked very hard at trying not to let it show.

Jessica smiled and hugged Audrey, thanking her for

being a true friend and reassuring her of her confidence. With great relief, Audrey picked up the large plate. When she turned to go, Jessica had disappeared, already on her way back to poolside.

The day didn't seem fun anymore for Audrey. Her arm was bothering her, and she was looking forward to the ride home.

CHAPTER

28

A friendless man is like a left hand without a right.

– Hebrew Proverb

"Play with me, Audrey," said Matthew, as he placed his dump truck and plastic people at Audrey's feet in the family room.

"Not now, Mattie, I want to watch T.V." Audrey answered her brother without taking her eyes off the movie she had put in the dvd player twenty minutes earlier.

Despite the five years between them, the siblings had always enjoyed a remarkable closeness. Alice Tabor was a wise mother in engaging her little daughter's assistance shortly after the birth of the new baby. As a consequence, Audrey had felt important, instead of pushed aside. Her helpfulness continued as Matthew began to walk and talk. When Audrey learned to read, she'd shared her picture stories with her brother. She discovered that building houses with Mattie's blocks or pushing his trucks around the apartment were great ways to pass the time on rainy afternoons. And it didn't take long for Mattie to see that his big sister was a good playmate and loyal friend.

But lately, Audrey had been paying less and less attention to Matthew, and now it seemed to him that something had changed.

"You said you'd play with me later. This is later. You don't play with me anymore! Come on, Audrey, let's play trucks. I'll be the fireman and you be the people," begged Matthew, pulling on his sister's pant leg as she munched on popcorn — unbuttered, of course.

"Look, Matthew, leave me alone!" screamed Audrey.

As Matthew began to plead one more time, Audrey knocked the plastic fireman out of her brother's hand, hurling it across the room, where it fell against a cast iron table leg.

As Matthew ran frantically to retrieve his toy, Audrey shrieked, "Get lost, and take your junk someplace else, Matthew!"

Holding his broken fireman, Matthew looked across the room in panic as his sister finished her tirade by kicking his yellow dump truck into the bookcase. He looked up at his sister and down at his favorite toys and cried. It was a sad little whimper that became a monstrous wail, and it seemed to have no stopping place.

It should have broken Audrey's heart; she loved Matthew

so. But on this day, Audrey had no heart to be broken. She felt nothing but anger and she didn't know why. What she did know was that she wanted to be left alone on the sofa, in the family room, in front of her movie. She was glad it was a rainy Saturday. It gave her an excuse to do nothing.

Sobbing and holding his broken toys, Matthew slowly climbed up the stairs to find his mother. Audrey resumed her vacant stare at the T.V. screen, hugging a pillow tightly to her chest.

"Audrey!" The voice was hard-edged and angry. Standing at the top of the basement stairs, in a tone of voice rarely heard in the Tabor household, her mother snapped, "Get up here now!"

Audrey slowly dragged herself up the flight. As she approached the kitchen doorway, she saw her mother kneeling by Mattie. She was drying his face and murmuring gently into his sad, wet eyes. When she looked up and saw Audrey, Mrs. Tabor handed her little boy one of a plateful of freshly baked brownies, and sweetly sent him back to the family room.

"What's going on with you and Mattie? He says you yelled at him and broke his toys on purpose!"

"Why do I have to play baby games if I don't want to? I'm sick of doing things I don't want to do. I wish everybody would just leave me alone!" Audrey shifted her feet and scratched her very aggravated rash that had now spread from a little below the shoulder to the bend in her arm.

"I've been noticing that you've been rubbing that arm of yours for the past week or so," said Mrs. Tabor. "Sit down, honey, and let me take a look."

Audrey replied, "Oh, I think it's probably a heat rash, or something. It's O.K." Mrs. Tabor knelt next to Audrey and pulled up her daughter's shirt sleeve. She was visibly appalled at what she saw. The skin on Audrey's upper arm had become bumpy and red and even bloody in some spots — the result of too much itching and scratching.

"Audrey, I'm making an appointment Monday morning with the doctor, and I will stay home to take you. I can't believe you have been suffering with this and not telling us." Mrs. Tabor paused for several seconds, and looked into Audrey's swimming eyes. "Is there anything else you're not telling us?" she asked quietly, as she held Audrey's hand.

She continued in as gentle a voice as she could manage. "Honey, I can't believe that you would treat your brother so badly. This is nothing like the Audrey we know. You didn't break his toys on purpose, did you?"

In the smallest voice Audrey ever spoke, she replied, "I didn't mean to break anything. I'm sorry." Unable to look into her mother's eyes, she looked at the floor. At that moment something caught in her, and she began to quietly cry.

Rising from her knees and pulling out a kitchen chair, Alice Tabor sat closely beside her weeping daughter. She took a slow, deep breath and began. "You said you wish everyone would just leave you alone. What do you mean? Are we bothering you somehow?"

Rubbing her arm, Audrey replied, "No. Nobody's bothering me. Everything's O.K." Mrs. Tabor didn't miss the fact that neither Audrey nor her arm were anything like O.K.

"Honey, you know that you mean everything to your brother. He just adores you, and you've always played so well together. Today you have really hurt his feelings, and he needs you to tell him how sorry you are."

"I know, Mom. I love Mattie, too. I'm just in a crummy mood I guess."

"Your Dad and I have noticed that you've been in a bad mood for a little while now — not just today."

"No, everything's great, really. Everything's great," Audrey answered quickly, trying to smile brightly.

Audrey assured her mother again that everything was fine, and her mother hugged her and told her that she loved her. Mrs. Tabor had been wondering if her daughter was suffering from the adolescent moodiness that she had heard so much about. She thought back to her own young years, and could remember only vaguely that there had been some hard times. But this rash and today's incident made her suspect that something far worse than moodiness might be going on with Audrey, and she resolved to find out what.

Audrey left, with great relief, to go to her room. At that moment, her mother made her an offer of a homemade brownie and a glass of milk. Stopping short, she was just about to sit down for one of her all time favorite snacks, when she thought better of it, and told her mom, no thanks.

Upstairs in her room, Audrey stood before the mirror and stared at herself. She saw a lot of people. She saw a chubby girl, an errand girl, an in-group girl, a sad girl, a nobody girl. How was it possible to feel so bad and not know why?

Leslie Koresky

CHAPTER 29

I would not live without the love of my friends.

– John Keats

"How's my favorite niece?" cried Aunt Bette as she walked toward the backyard, where Audrey and her mother were setting out plastic and paper for the family cookout. In her arms was a large round plastic container that Audrey hoped was her Aunt's amazingly delicious chocolate chip cake. Audrey truly believed the dessert could win first prize in any baking contest, maybe even beating out Lindsay's mocha cake. Coming up just behind Aunt Bette were Uncle Frank and Beth. Beth was holding a small wrapped gift and waving at Matthew, who was running toward them at breakneck speed.

On this last Sunday in July, the Tabors and the Frasiers were about to enjoy a back yard barbecue under a perfect, cloudless sky. Tom Tabor had spent all day Saturday mowing the lawn, cleaning up the yard, and polishing up his beloved

182

new gas grill. Audrey remembered the warm April day when the family trekked to the New Hampshire warehouse in pursuit of "Tom's Magic Cooking Machine," as Alice Tabor teasingly called it. Since the time they had moved into their house at the beginning of the year, all Audrey's dad seemed to talk about was getting a grill. It had become a Sunday morning ritual for him to browse through the newspaper circulars — marking pages, making notes, and mumbling about various grilling features. Audrey's mom would make an impressive display of interest with remarks like, "Can it really do all that, honey?" or "Oh, isn't that nice." It was like pretending to be excited when Mattie vroomed his trucks and said, "Look how fast I can go!" Then, again, maybe her mom was really interested… parents could be so strange.

The grill Tom Tabor lovingly placed into their van that day was, according to the future grill-master himself, a real super duper. It had two levels for grilling, a tray on each side for plates, cup holders, and shelving for cooking utensils, and it could cook enough meat to serve Audrey's entire class. The contraption apparently included everything but a dvd player and a cell phone. Since the beginning of the summer season, the Tabors cooked weekend meals on the grill, and some dinners during the week if Audrey's dad got home early enough. But for today's lunch, Tom Tabor could barely contain his excitement. It was his first chance to show off his greatly perfected one-handed meat flipping skills, which he learned from studying Bob Diamond, the Tabors' next-door neighbor. It was neighborhood knowledge that Bob and his grill did not part until the first frost.

Matthew wrapped his arms around Beth's legs as she kissed him on his head. A second or two later Uncle Frank was lifting Mattie up on his shoulders for a ride.

"Frank!" shouted Aunt Bette. "You'll hurt your back, for heaven's sake."

Frank ignored the warning and continued to carry his giggling nephew until they got to the back yard.

It was a wonderful day. Now that Tom was a proud homeowner, he and Frank discussed home maintenance, property values, and of course, barbecuing. Everyone complimented Tom and Alice on the meal of chicken, hotdogs, corn, and homemade potato salad. Aunt Bette's cake was, indeed, chocolate chip. Everyone had double helpings of everything — except Audrey, who ate one piece of chicken, one half of one ear of corn, and none of her mother's potato salad, which had always been among her favorite dishes. Instead of sweetened iced tea, she drank a glass of water with lemon. She completed her meal with a single forkful of her favorite cake, and turned down the offer of vanilla ice cream. Audrey's eating behavior was not lost on her mother, whose brow furrowed with concern.

Audrey helped her mother carry some things back into the house, while her aunt and cousin gathered up the trash bag.

Placing the ketchup and mustard back into the fridge, Mrs. Tabor said, "Audrey, I don't think you're eating enough these days."

"What do you mean?" answered Audrey.

"I watched you eat lunch today. You barely ate any chicken, no rolls, and no hot dogs, which have always been your favorite. You didn't even take a spoonful of my potato salad. But the last straw was when you hardly ate any of Aunt Belle's cake. I remember when you couldn't get enough of it. And this is not the first time I've noticed your new eating habits. You are a growing girl, and need to eat enough of everything to stay strong and healthy."

"Well, if I keep eating all the fattening food that everyone throws at me, I sure will be growing — growing into a fat, ugly girl that no one wants to be seen with. I suppose you'd be happy if I looked like Alisha Kranz! You can't make me eat all this junk!"

"*Fat?*" cried Mrs. Tabor, eyes wide with shock. "Do you honestly think that you're *fat?* Actually, Audrey, have you looked in the mirror lately? Your clothes are loose on you, and your face looks too thin. Can you honestly stand there and tell me that you are afraid of being fat? And who is this person you mentioned?"

"Alisha Kranz is fat and ugly and everyone laughs at her and I'm going to be fat, too, if I don't start watching what I eat. You're my mother and you'd say I was beautiful no matter what

I looked like. Why should I believe you anyway?"

"Audrey, where are you getting these ideas? You never sounded like this before. Is it those girls you've been hanging around with? Do they tell you that you're fat?"

"Maybe I sound like this now because I'm finally growing up, and you don't like it that I'm not your little baby anymore who does everything she's told!" Audrey's voice was becoming louder, angrier, and more shrill.

Mrs. Tabor watched Audrey as she rubbed her right arm. "Audrey, have you been using the medication that the doctor prescribed for your rash?"

The previous week, Dr. Farrell had prescribed a cream for her arm, which was supposed to take away the itch and dry up the rash. He diagnosed her condition as some minor skin irritation, which he said appears on some people for little reason. Audrey's had become severely irritated because of too much scratching.

"Stop nagging me! I can take care of myself! I'm not a helpless baby!"

Now Audrey's mother's voice was beginning to get louder and angrier, as well. "You seem to accuse me a lot lately of treating you like a baby. Frankly, as long as you act like a baby I'll treat you like one. I swear, I'll force feed you if I have to. I will not stand around and watch you disappear into some sick stick figure who thinks she's too fat! Those girls better not be the cause of this. If they're putting these ideas into your head, I'll give them a piece of my mind!"

Audrey screamed, "Oh my God! If you ever talked to my friends like that I'd never speak to you again. My friends love me. They're great and I'm having the best summer ever. Why don't you get with the program and leave me alone!"

Beth and her mother had heard the noise from outside and hurried to the house to find out what was wrong. At the last part of Audrey's horrible tirade, they entered the kitchen to find both Alice and Audrey in tears. In all the years they had known Audrey, never had they heard or witnessed such a display of anger. Alice shook her head helplessly at Bette, looking as though she had just been slapped. Audrey turned quickly on her heel to leave and made it halfway up the stairs when her cousin caught up with her.

"Hey, Audrey, you O.K.?" said Beth, as she placed her hand on her shoulder.

Audrey stopped and looked at her favorite cousin. "My mother is driving me crazy. She nags and criticizes me all the time. I can't stand it!"

"Do you want to go for a walk? You can talk to me while I take a look at your beautiful neighborhood. Deal?"

Audrey nodded, and followed Beth out the front door. Before they started their walk, Beth ran back inside to let her Aunt Alice know that they would be out for a while.

Arbor Road was part of a quiet neighborhood, lined with maple trees and modest homes of both one and two levels. A few were of multi-level design. Some had garages, some front porches. Yards were dotted with children's bikes and playhouses. Gardens were manicured in some, poorly tended in others. It was a comfortable, friendly place. As they strolled along, they passed a small group of young children making chalk drawings on the street. Further ahead were three teenagers shooting baskets in a driveway.

"This kind of reminds me of where we live. Except we don't have as big a yard. You must like living in the suburbs, huh?" said Beth.

"Yeah, it's nice. I like it here. It's great having such a nice room and a yard and everything," answered Audrey. "But this is nothing compared to where my friends live."

"Say, how is Gretchen doing, anyway?" asked Beth. She had remembered Audrey speaking about the friend that she made shortly after having moved into Greenwood Springs.

"Oh, no. I mean, we're actually not friendly anymore. I hang out with another group of girls — Lindsay and Jessica and their group. I haven't seen Gretchen in a while."

"How come?" The girls turned left onto Garden Road and continued. Audrey waved at a neighbor tending her flowers.

"When I started getting friendly with Lindsay and her friends, I tried to include Gretchen, but she didn't like them and I guess they didn't like her either. I really tried, but Gretchen didn't want me hanging around with them and we had a fight. So, anyway, I've been going almost every day to Lindsay and Jessica's club. It's been great."

"You mean, like a clubhouse, or something?" asked Beth.

"No," Audrey explained. "It's their country club. We use the pool and have lunch and snacks. And their moms play tennis and their dads play golf on the weekends. It's cool."

"Audrey, why were you so mad at your mom before?" asked Beth.

"She's trying to keep me fat. She was angry just because I didn't have big stupid helpings of everything at the table. I need to lose weight, and she's not helping. She's says I'm too thin. Can you believe it? I'm so blubbery in my bathing suit." Audrey laughed sarcastically.

"You know, Audrey, I don't think she actually wants you to be fat. And, by the way, not only are you not fat, you're kind of too thin. Now don't be mad at me, but haven't you noticed how loose your clothes are on you?"

Secretly, Beth was worried about the way her cousin's face was beginning to appear — sunken under her cheekbones and pale in color. Her pretty green eyes had lost their usual sparkle, and underneath them were dark shadows.

"Lindsay says I have great bones. All I need is to lose a few pounds and I'll be perfect. She's totally perfect, and so is Jessica. You should see their clothes, Beth. And their houses. They actually like me and want me in their group," emphasized Audrey.

"Well," answered Beth, "if this Lindsay liked you so much, she'd like you just the way you are, which is beautiful. And, Audrey, you have never ever been too fat!"

Audrey was silent. She loved Beth and didn't want to fight with her. But her cousin just didn't get it. Nobody did. The conversation turned to other things.

"So," asked Beth, looking for more comfortable territory, "reading any good books this summer?"

When Audrey answered that she hadn't been reading at all except for gossip and fashion magazines, Beth tried not to show her surprise. All the visits Audrey would make to the library, trading one book for another, week after week, not to mention the books borrowed from Beth's own collection. And the times they would even try writing their own short stories just for fun…where had it all gone?

"Audrey," she said. " You used to talk anout having a little garden full of your favorite flowers. Have you thought about starting one?"

Audrey turned to face her cousin. "Oh, Beth," she replied with digust. "That was just a dumb idea and you know it. I can't be digging in the dirt — I would ruin my nail polish. You need to get with the program!"

Lilabeth Frasier was dumbfounded by the disdain in Audrey's voice. What was happening to her cousin? Beth feared that she knew, but she couldn't be sure.

By the time they returned to the Tabors', Audrey had

cooled down. Her mom and dad were sitting on the back porch with Aunt Alice and Uncle Frank, and Mattie was half asleep in the rocking chair.

By eight-thirty, the Frasiers gave their goodbye and thank you hugs, and placed their leftover food packages in the back seat of the car. As her parents slid into the front seat, Beth came close to Audrey and, in a low voice, said, "Audrey, you told me how much your friends like you. But I was wondering...Do you like them?"

Audrey jumped and was just about to answer when Beth kissed her goodbye and hurried into her family's car.

Audrey walked through the back porch and looked at Mattie, now sleeping soundly in the rocking chair, his little feet dangling over the edge of the big wooden seat. She felt tired, too, and went up to her room. While putting together an outfit for the next day, she heard the phone ring downstairs. Several minutes later, her mother knocked on her door. Audrey was afraid that her mom was planning on continuing their earlier fight, and therefore, was already annoyed when she opened the door.

Mrs. Tabor looked as though she had been crying. She spoke with difficulty. "That was Irene Hart. She is very worried. Gretchen has been hospitalized for depression. I thought you should know."

Her mother turned away and quietly closed her door, leaving Audrey standing in the middle of her room.

CHAPTER
30

A faithful friend is the medicine of life.

– *Ecclesiastes 6:16*

August began with a series of gloomy, drizzly days. Audrey wanted to see Gretchen but was secretly relieved when she was told that her friend wasn't allowed visitors yet. She didn't want to admit it to herself, but she was greatly embarrassed about the way their friendship had ended — not, of course, that it was Audrey's fault. After all, she had tried to include Gretchen, hadn't she? It was Gretchen who made it so impossible, right? Audrey continued to play the scenario in her head, like a video on rewind. But she knew that neither her version nor Gretchen's version of the story made much difference now…

On this dreary Wednesday, the Style Girls congregated at Hillary's house. The girls were lounging comfortably, and shoelessly, in the family room. Jessica was stretched out on one end of the well-used navy blue sectional sofa, flipping aimlessly through a magazine; Lindsay was at the other end, moving in time to the music on her iPod; Brianna and Hillary were slouched together in the middle, feet stretched out onto the large ottoman, texting. Audrey, the last to arrive that morning, was curled up in the deep red double-sized chair that faced the sofa. On the ottoman and the floor were strewn an enormous number of celebrity and fashion magazines and at least twenty-five dvds. Bottles of nail polish in every color of the rainbow, and beyond, were lined up on one of the end tables, along with various hair accessories.

Jessica said, "All right, everybody. Cell phones in a pile; Audrey doesn't have one, and we can't sit around all day texting." Brianna, Hillary, Lindsay, and Jessica all tossed their cell phones into a pile on the ottoman. All Audrey could think about was how her parents refused to let her have one until she got a little older. It was becoming a real sore point at home: one more thing that her parents just didn't understand.

Even though Hillary's house was not as grand as Jessica's or Lindsay's, the family room was a comfortable extension of the kitchen. The sofa, loveseat, and chairs were arranged for easy viewing of the 50-inch flat screen T.V., below which was a cabinet holding all kinds of electronic equipment and an impressive collection of movies. Hillary's family loved to watch movies, which they preferred over most T.V. programs.

And Hillary's father was as obsessed with electronics as Audrey's dad was with barbecue grills. When Mr. Wright wasn't reading history books, he was pouring over electronics magazines, always keeping himself informed of the latest technological development. For example, in the family room cabinet was, according to Hillary, a sound system that Mr. Wright had singlehandedly connected throughout the house. Her mom had wanted to hire a professional electrician, but her dad loved to do things himself and didn't want to spend more money than necessary. His second floor office, which Audrey glimpsed in passing, was outfitted with the latest in computers, plus an all-in-one printer/copier/scanner/fax, and 42-inch T.V. Every member of the family had a tablet and a cell phone, with ear buds, and all the latest internet connection technology. Hillary said that her mom wished they could have a real home theater, but her dad had drawn the line there.

"Too bad," Hillary had said. "Imagine how cool that would be. But dad says we can always watch whatever we want on the family room T.V."

Audrey couldn't understand how anybody would want more than what the Wright family already had. And then Audrey remembered the comment Hillary had made during one of their shopping excursions: that it's important to dress well. Maybe some people just needed to look up-to-date and perfect all the time.

On a wall adjacent to the sofa was a bay window, upon

which were crowded family pictures and knicknacks from various trips. There were shells from Bermuda, Mickey Mouse collectables from Disney World, driftwood from Nantucket. Any remaining space was taken up by houseplants and flowers from Mrs. Wright's back yard garden, which could be seen through this window. Today, the usually sunny, colorful view was awash in gray, maple and oak leaves dripping, daisies and asters sad and soggy, wicker-style chairs drenched and runny on a patio of puddled pink stone. After the rain, the flowers would be all the more full and rich for their long drink of water; but for now, the little garden was damp, dull, and dreary. This was the fourth dull day, and the girls were beginning to droop like the leaves on the bowed trees.

It was nearly eleven in the morning. After putting away the dishes from the dishwasher and quickly going over the counters, Hillary's mother left for the hairdresser and a game of indoor tennis with Mrs. Morton, Jessica's mom.

At the sound of the closing door, the house was beautifully quiet. When Hillary suggested they pop some corn everyone dropped whatever they were doing and happily made their way into the spotless kichen.

Hillary pulled down a box of microwave popping corn, and opened the clear wrap on two individual packages. Brianna was moving through the cabinets like someone who knew her way around a room, finding two large bowls. Audrey was employed to get the lemonade from the fridge, and

Lindsay and Jessica were instructed to find napkins. Ten minutes later, bowls and napkins assembled, the girls were back in the family room crowded around two steaming bowls of freshly popped corn.

Suddenly, the sound of a strumming guitar interrupted the crunching. It took a few seconds for the girls to realize that it was one of the cell phones. Recognizing the ring, Jessica grabbed her phone.

Hungrily stuffing handfuls of the freshly popped treat into their mouths, the girls were paying little to no attention to the ensuing phone conversation, until the tone changed dramatically.

"What do you mean?" said Jessica, now sitting straight as a light pole on the edge of the sofa.

Audrey, munching away, was listening as nonchalantly as she could while watching out of the corner of her eye.

"But you promised! You said we'd all go!" continued a very agitated Jessica, now standing up and walking toward the kitchen.

Lindsay was following Jessica's movements with a look of deep concern for her friend. Hillary and Brianna exchanged glances. Audrey didn't look at anyone.

The drama continued.

In a voice becoming snappish and whining Jessica pleaded, "You always break your promises! You don't care about me anyway — just your old, boring tennis friends and charity idiots!"

There was a momentary silence, most likely while Jessica's mother was taking her turn to speak. Then came the sound of Jessica's angry voice.

"Well, when Daddy comes home Monday from his trip, he'll —"

Her response was interrupted. When she spoke again it sounded choked and unclear.

"Yes, he is too coming home! You're lying! I hate you!"

The phone confrontation was over, and the family room gathering was eerily silent. Audrey could hear a fly buzzing against the window and the faint barking of a dog in a faraway neighbor's yard. It was several minutes before Jessica returned. Her eyes were puffy and red-rimmed, and her face was set hard.

In a quiet and gentle voice, Lindsay interrupted the stillness of the room.

"Are you O.K., Jess?"

Jessica responded to her friend icily, "Why don't you mind your own business for a change, Lindsay?"

Lindsay seemed to grow smaller in her chair, nearly disappearing from the rest of the group.

Mercifully breaking the uncomfortable silence, Hillary looked up and quickly blurted, "Tyra DeAngelo would like to join our group."

"So," scowled Jessica, "who wouldn't?"

All the girls laughed nervously.

"Who is Tyra DeAngelo?" asked Lindsay.

Hillary explained. "You know her. She's the one with the long black hair. Her clothes are totally cool. She moved here at the beginning of the year from Florida. She's smart, and even though she just moved to town, she seems to know what's going on. Her dad knows some senators and stuff. I had a nice talk with her a few days ago at Davis' Ice Cream. I like her."

Taking a long drink of lemonade and then putting down her drink, Jessica responded darkly, "You know the drill. We'll put her through the ropes in September, and see if she makes it."

"Cool!" exclaimed Hillary.

Audrey wondered what Jessica meant by "the ropes." They all nodded, like it was something they did all the time. She began to wonder what ropes she herself was put through…

"What movie are we watching today? I've got *Spiderman*," said Brianna, with a mouth full of popcorn.

Lindsay waited to swallow, and then answered emphatically, "I just saw that and I don't want to see it again so soon."

"I brought the new *Sound of Music*," offered Audrey. It was her favorite musical, and she loved every version of it.

As if Audrey hadn't spoken, Hillary said, "I think we should all watch this." She held up an R-rated horror movie. The cover displayed the gruesome picture of a blood-drenched knife with the face of a screaming woman in the background.

"Oh," said Lindsay, softly, "I don't know about that. It looks really scary."

Added a disturbed Audrey, "My mom would never let me watch that movie."

Any more than she would let me have a cell phone, she thought grumpily. But secretly, she was just a little bit relieved that her mother wouldn't let her see such movies. They were a lot worse than her old favorite, *Poltergeist*. And that thought made her think about Milly. She still hadn't called her.

"Well, your mom isn't here, is she?" Hillary said this as she looked to Brianna for approval. Brianna sneered. Audrey looked down and tried to disappear as Lindsay had a few moments before.

Jessica finally entered the debate. "Well, I saw it with my older sister, and it was no big deal. I'm up for it."

Lindsay readily agreed, which left only Audrey.

"I don't think I should. I mean, I don't feel right watching this without my parents' permission."

"So, what are you saying — that you want to go home?" asked Lindsay, who seemed to be losing patience.

"Her parents are working," said Hillary, as if Audrey were not in the room. "There's nobody to take her home. Isn't that right, Audrey?"

As Audrey nodded, Jessica spoke up, "Come on Audrey. Don't ruin this for everyone. Stop being a baby and get with the program. Everyone wants to see this movie. What's so hard about going along, anyway?"

At that, Lindsay gave Jessica a high five and Hillary put the movie into the machine.

After nearly two long hours of horrifying threats, stabbings, and ugly music, the movie was mercifully over. Audrey, who had no experience watching movies of this sort, viewed most of the film either between the fingers of her hands or partially behind a tightly clutched pillow. Ten minutes into the story the popcorn and lemonade had lost their flavor.

After lunch, which consisted of delivery pizza, the girls decided to experiment with their vast selection of nail polishes — the Style Girls' collection. While painting their nails, the conversation turned to the subject of Lindsay.

"So, Linds," said Brianna, blowing on her right hand and inspecting for flaws, "You'd better watch it. I saw you eat three pieces of pizza. We'll be calling you Miss Chubbs pretty soon at the pool!"

"Yeah," said Hillary, smiling, "Pretty soon Audrey will be looking better than you in her bathing suit. I saw Richard Nelson noticing her last week."

Richard Nelson was considered by any girl who had any taste at all to be the most gorgeous boy anywhere. He was tall, with blue eyes and very dark brown hair, and was incredibly tanned from spending his time either at the pool or at his family's second home on Nantucket. And he was an "older man" of almost thirteen. The girls his own age were always hanging around him, trying to make conversation, or showing off in the pool, trying to get him to notice. Audrey was astonished and embarrassed at Hillary's suggestion that Richard was watching her. And what's more, she felt very uncomfortable at the suggestion that she was in some way better than Lindsay.

Joining in, Jessica, warned her friend, "Oh, no, Linds, cottage cheese for you!"

It was the most awful thing they could have said to Lindsay, who was visibly shaken.

"Oh really?" answered Lindsay angrily. "Well, Hillary, I wouldn't talk, if I were you. I've never seen you leave any food on your plate. By the time you get to high school you'll look like Alisha, and then it won't matter how well dressed and smart you are!"

"I think, personally," offered Brianna, "that Hillary probably won't have to worry about any of that. She looks great no matter what she eats." Brianna and Hillary smiled at each other.

Lindsay came back at Brianna. "What do you know about anything, Brianna?"

"What's that supposed to mean?" asked Brianna, setting down her nail polish brush.

"You hung around with a bunch of losers before we took you into our group. You wouldn't know a hairbrush from a paintbrush without my personal help. And my family knows more important people in this town than almost anyone. Please, Brianna, if it weren't for Hillary, who you seem to be glued onto, you'd be lost. And by the way, Hillary, a boy like Richard Nelson wouldn't look at someone like you if you were the last girl left in the world." With the last insult, Lindsay left to get herself more lemonade.

Furious at the remark, Hillary followed Lindsay into the kitchen and continued the argument.

"Well, at least Brianna and I don't bake cakes and give people half the recipes so they get all ruined!" Hillary's smile was mean and self-satisfied.

Audrey, sitting as still as death, wanted to bury herself in the floor. Jessica was never supposed to have told that to anybody. Audrey had trusted her to keep the information to herself. She thought she was her friend. Now Audrey was in trouble and she had never meant to hurt Lindsay's feelings.

Lindsay yelled for Audrey, who immediately appeared in the kitchen. Hillary stood and watched. Almost immediately, the girls were joined by Jessica and Brianna.

"You just gossip about me to my friends? I thought you and I were friends, Audrey, after all I've done for you! "

Turning smugly to Hillary, Lindsay said, "Well, Hillary, I understand that you've been bad-mouthing me pretty nicely."

"I have not! If anyone said that then they're lying!"

"Jessica would never make things up, and she told me

that Audrey told her that you called me a bragger. And, not only that, Audrey told Jessica that you and Audrey never planned way ahead of time to dress alike. You did that on purpose, knowing that I'd show up in the dress we were supposed to wear together. You did it to be mean. And you," continued Lindsay, now looking at Audrey, "you lied right along with Hillary!"

Audrey's mind flashed back quickly to both the day at the club when Jessica asked about Hillary, and the day at school when Audrey covered up Hillary's lie. But she never meant anything mean. She trusted Jessica, and she didn't want to make any trouble that day in the schoolyard for Hillary. How did this all happen?

Audrey tried to explain. "Lindsay, please believe me. I never meant to hurt your feelings. I wasn't trying to be mean. I guess I did the wrong thing. I'm so sorry. You've been a really good friend." She was fighting hard to hold back tears that she was afraid would become an embarrassing flood. And she was terrified that Lindsay might reveal what she knew about Audrey's changing clothes in the girls' room at school.

Before Lindsay could respond, Jessica spoke.

"OK, guys. This has gone far enough. Let's take a break before anyone says anything else."

The girls sat quietly around the kitchen table. After a few minutes, Hillary and Brianna walked back into the family room and played another selection from the iPod that they had hooked into Mr. Wright's sound system. The heavy baseline began to beat relentlessly. Lindsay stared angrily at Audrey, as Jessica sat between them trying to calm everyone's nerves. She reminded Lindsay that Audrey made a very sweet apology, and Lindsay responded by shrugging her shoulders and looking out the window. Audrey wiped her eyes with the back of her hand.

By the time mothers appeared in the driveway to pick up daughters, the girls had tentatively made up, although the latter part of the afternoon had remained uncharacteristically quiet.

CHAPTER

31

…the most liberal profession of good-will
is very far from being the surest mark of it.
– *George Washington*

August dragged on, and Gretchen seemed to come into Audrey's mind more and more. She still hadn't been allowed to visit Gretchen, who had been in the hospital for — Audrey thought it seemed like forever.

"She's been there so long. Could I just see her, even for a little bit?"

Audrey was moving her breakfast cereal around her bowl, eating practically nothing, drinking almost none of her orange juice, which was now unappetizingly warm.

It was the first time Audrey had actually inquired about Gretchen, and Mrs. Tabor, while encouraged, needed to proceed delicately. Leaving the dishes in the sink, she pulled up a chair across from Audrey and spoke.

"Honey, do you know what 'depression' is?"

"Yeah, it's when you're sad, right?"

"Well, yes, basically. I mean that's part of it."

Twisting her wedding ring around her finger while staring blankly at the wall clock, Mrs. Tabor was trying to figure out the best way to help her daughter understand.

"We can feel sad when we read a sad story or watch a movie about unhappy things. Even in our own lives we can have moments, even days of feeling bad, maybe when we get a poor grade, or lose a pet. We can be terribly disappointed when we don't get to do something we've been looking forward to."

Audrey interjected, "You mean like when we didn't get to go New York that summer like Daddy promised?"

Mrs. Tabor smiled, "Yes, like that." Sitting up a little straighter, she continued.

"Well, real depression is different. The sadness is very deep and it can make a person become extremely sick. And it's not from just one disappointing thing. It is so deep that a person may not be able to find a way out of it by herself. Sometimes skilled doctors have to work very hard and long to figure out why a person is so sick and how to make her better."

Audrey could barely feel herself breathe, so still was her body. A neighbor's dog was barking, a truck was screeching by, but she heard nothing, nothing but her mother's words.

"So they won't let me see Gretchen because she's too sick?" Audrey's eyes were wide with panic as she whispered, "Mom, is Gretchen going to die?"

Grabbing her daughter's hands Mrs. Tabor answered quickly, "No! Audrey, no! Mrs. Hart told me she is getting stronger. The doctors are encouraged that she will recover. Gretchen feels she needs more time before she sees friends, that's all. *She* needs to feel well enough. We need to respect her wishes."

Audrey was relieved that Gretchen was better, but Audrey's mom had used the word, "friend," and she didn't feel like much of a friend.

Audrey's summer schedule continued with her being dropped off at Lindsay's in the morning, either to stay there on rainy days, or hang out at the club on fair weather days. A few times during the vacation, Mrs. Brentoff dropped the girls off at the movies and afterward took them out for ice cream. Poolside lunches, movies, ice cream, daily friends — for anybody, it would be a dream summer vacation. For a while, it had certainly seemed that way to Audrey. But since the disaster at Hillary's house, Audrey was finding herself less enthusiastic each morning as she rose and dressed for the day.

The odd thing was that for everyone else, it was "business as usual" — the same silly chatter, gossip, and jokes. No one seemed to be angry anymore, and no one appeared to be upset with Audrey. On the one hand, she thought it was a good thing that the girls held no grudges. Her parents always said that it was unhealthy to carry a grudge. But Audrey still couldn't shake the idea that her confidences had been betrayed, and more than once. Wasn't that a bad thing? She wanted to be angry, but she wanted to be friends, too.

There remained many beautiful late summer days, when the sky looked like puffs of white cotton sitting on light blue linen. On one such day, Hillary was telling a story that made everyone laugh hilariously — while Audrey was dozing in the sun. The story was followed later by the group's usual pastime of people watching. When comments were traded by the girls, Audrey was flipping through a magazine. After lunch, when asked to find some extra towels, Audrey declined, answering she that she was tired.

Jessica approached Audrey and sat beside her on her chaise while Hillary, Brianna, and Lindsay were in the pool.

"Hey, girlfriend, what's up today?"

For the first time, Jessica's "girlfriend" salutation annoyed Audrey. She wasn't feeling like Jessica's girlfriend any more than she was feeling like Hillary's best buddy.

Answering, Audrey said, "What do you mean? Nothing's up."

"Well, I mean, you haven't been with us at all today. Hillary's joke about the boys in the pool was hilarious, and you're, like, sleeping, or something. And all Brianna asked for was a couple of extra towels. Are you feeling O.K.?"

"What's wrong with not getting up every ten minutes to go on errands for everyone? Maybe I'd like to relax, too," said Audrey, with a slight edge to her voice.

Jessica had an exaggeratedly shocked expression on her face. "Whoa, Audrey. This is a disturbing side of you I've never seen!"

"What's so disturbing about not wanting to be the gofer all the time or being angry when people break promises and tell stories?"

Jessica suddenly became calm and thoughtful. She began slowly and quietly, "Oh, I think I know what this is all about. You're angry about what happened at Hillary's last week, aren't you?"

"Why shouldn't I be?"

"Look, around here stuff like that happens all the time. It was just the first time you saw it. We're all used to it, and nobody really cares after a while. Sometimes we just have our days when we pick on somebody, and then it gets out of hand, that's all. Hey, you gotta be tough to be a Style Girl. You just gotta get with the program, Aud — and *SMILE!* It's still summer!" Jessica ended her speech by giving Audrey a mock punch in the shoulder.

As Jessica got up, she said, "Hey, Audrey, that arm is totally gross, you know? You ought to do something about it. After all, you do wear a bathing suit every day. Maybe more cream, or something…"

Audrey was mortified. What was she thinking? She should have covered the stinging, itchy mess. It had not cleared; in fact it was worsening, spreading down her arm toward her wrist. As soon as she returned to her chaise at the pool she began to rummage through her beach bag for the pink shirt she brought in case of cooler weather. While the girls splashed around she quickly put it on.

After the girls got out of the pool, they seemed as friendly as ever with Audrey. She supposed Jessica was right. The fight never really meant anything. They all seemed to still like Audrey. Maybe she was making too much out of nothing. But as she sat and scratched her irritated, sore arm, it occurred to her that Jessica caused as much trouble as Hillary and she never apologized either. Apparently, no one in the group found it necessary to apologize for anything.

It was strange the things that could suddenly pop into a person's head. Audrey was imagining Milly sitting beside her and they were watching these country club girls and playing the "Name Game." Lindsay was Miss Ponytail, and who was Jessica? Well, maybe the "Name Game" might not be such fun anymore, but she and Milly would be able to find new ways to make each other laugh. They always had. She wondered what Milly was doing at that moment. And what about Gretchen? Would she ever be O.K., and would she ever want to see Audrey? Something about Gretchen's illness really scared her.

Staring off across the thick greenery, looking at nothing, Audrey began to silently weep — just little tears and not long enough to attract attention. Sunglasses helped until the tears went away.

Late in the day, Brianna suggested that they all jump in the pool for one last game. The beach balls and other paraphernalia were nowhere to be seen, and Hillary told Audrey to please go locate them. Audrey was about to get up when she changed her mind and suggested that perhaps Hillary would like to find them herself. It seemed to Audrey that in that instant all sound and movement was suspended. Lindsay looked at Hillary, who glanced at Brianna, who glared at Audrey, who crossed her legs and fixed the elastic in her ponytail. And then all turned to Jessica as she spoke.

"Hillary, why don't you try to find the stuff? Lindsay and Brianna and I will wait for you in the pool."

As the girls jumped or playfully pushed each other into the water, Audrey realized that her friends didn't seem interested in including her in their final swim of the day.

CHAPTER
32

Love your neighbor as yourself.

– *Leviticus 10:18*

During the last week of August, Audrey's parents took vacation time. Audrey didn't care that it was a "stay-cation" and that they wouldn't be going away anywhere. She was happy not to have to get up early enough to be dropped off at Lindsay's. She also felt relieved to be home in her own space to do what she wanted to do. It was hard to believe, but a person could actually get tired of the pool. Her mom used some of the time to do housework that she didn't get to do during the week and the rest for reading and relaxing. Her dad repaired his broken lawnmower and did some small carpentry jobs around the house that he enjoyed: new shelves in the family room; a new closet door for Matthew. Matthew had made friends with another five-year-old who lived three doors down. Throughout any given day, their play site alternated between the Tabor residence and the Eliot household. Adam Eliot was a nice little boy, and the Tabors were fond of the family.

Mrs. Tabor thought the down time at home would do Audrey some good, but remained concerned at her continued moodiness and poor eating habits. Even Lilabeth had called her aunt to say that she was worried about Audrey.

When she wasn't snapping at her family, Audrey was quiet and withdrawn. In addition, her arm wasn't clearing up and she was looking thin and pale. Family dinners, eaten on the back porch, usually consisted of grilled chicken or hamburgers, salad, sweet corn fresh from a nearby farm, and rolls. Occasionally, Mrs. Tabor served dessert. Audrey's portions seemed to be getting smaller and smaller, and her rash angrier and angrier.

One morning, Audrey was flipping through the channels on the remote, looking for nothing in particular, when her mom, folding laundry at a nearby table, made a suggestion.

"You know, honey, I was thinking. Why don't you and I get dressed and make a day of it? I'll take you out for lunch and buy you some new clothes for school. How does that sound? We haven't done much together in a long time. And while we're out, we'll go by Dr. Farrell's and he'll check your arm again. And maybe, if we have time tonight, we'll get a sitter for Mattie and you and Dad and I can go to a movie. I think there are a couple of movies you wanted to see."

Alice Tabor had already made the appointment with the

doctor but wanted to sound casual about it, and thought that if it were part of a fun day, Audrey wouldn't protest. Audrey was protesting a lot these days, and it was hard on the family.

Mrs. Tabor was relieved and surprised that her idea went over as well as it did. And the day proved to be wonderful fun for both mother and daughter. At least most of it did.

At about ten in the morning, they left the house and Alice Tabor eased her car out toward the center of Greenwood Springs. They drove past an imposing granite statue of an early American war hero, flanked by three wooden benches and two large maple trees, on the town green. Once a common pasture for the livestock of early residents, the green was now hosting scattered picnickers and sun worshippers. Alice mentioned to Audrey that it might be nice for the Tabor family to take a picnic out there some weekend. Audrey looked out the car window, but didn't seem to see anything.

Alice drove on through town toward the highway and resolved to offer Audrey a treat to wrap up the day when they were finished shopping. The town's most delicious attractions were Davis' Ice Cream Stand and Kramer's Kandy Shoppe. Davis' Ice Cream stood on a knoll at Davis' Dairy Farm near the outskirts of town, which, to the delight of children, came complete with mooing cows, a duck pond, and a petting zoo. Kramer's Kandy Shoppe was famous and had nearly a monopoly during holidays. The original owner, Helen Kramer, had started the business in about 1932 with her own patented recipes for whipped fruits covered in homemade chocolate. Her granddaughter had continued that tradition into the present, adding some of her own chocolate magic. Today, however, Alice thought Audrey might opt for ice cream.

The mall lay outside the town limits, just a short ride up the highway. Even though it was a suburban shopping mall, it made Audrey think of the times she and her mom had spent browsing through Boston stores and having fun lunches in noisy little restaurants. It made her think of their strolls through the colorful Public Garden and the quiet, lazy rides on her beloved Swan Boats. Audrey was also remembering Milly, and the way they used to compare their problems to see which one was worse. Milly's tenth birthday had long since come and gone and Audrey had never called. She sank more deeply into her seat and her thoughts.

Alice Tabor parked in the mall's lot and mother and daughter proceeded into the entrance. Although it didn't have the charm and elegance of Boston's Newbury Street, at least it had a variety of shops with clothing for young people that both Audrey and her mother could agree on. The two shoppers made their way through three department stores and two boutiques. The outing took a lot longer than either Audrey or her mother would have anticipated. Audrey asked to try things on alone in the dressing rooms, and then come out and model for her mother. It seemed that the countless skirts, tops, and pants that Audrey had chosen were far too big, hanging limply over thin shoulders and narrow hips. After a few attempts at different styles and ever smaller sizes, Audrey and Mrs. Tabor decided on four new outfits and two pairs of shoes. She didn't think she could recall ever seeing her mother so generous and so unconcerned about the price of things.

As they exited the final store, Audrey stopped to hug her mom and thank her for all her beautiful things that she could hardly wait to wear. But Alice Tabor's heart nearly stopped at the thinness of her child's body. In her arms were many folds of clothing and very little girl. Holding this fragile child in her arms, she was sure that something had gone terribly wrong. She was glad that Dr. Farrell would be examining Audrey later that day. Maybe he would know what to do.

Although excited about her new clothes, Audrey remained quiet and thoughtful as she nibbled distractedly on her club sandwich and chips. Gretchen was lying in the hospital sick. Maybe Alisha was with her. Audrey couldn't help but think that Alisha was a better friend to Gretchen than she was. And who, she wondered, was Milly's best friend now?

"You must be looking forward to starting school, honey," commented Mrs. Tabor between sips of iced tea. She watched her daughter as she barely made a dent in her food, but did not comment further.

"Yeah, I guess," answered Audrey.

"Well, Audrey, those clothes look terrific on you. You

will be this fall's sensation! The girls will be so impressed!" she joked.

"Yeah, thanks, Mom. They're really great. I can't believe you let me get so much!" Audrey smiled quickly and just as quickly stared off into space.

Mrs. Tabor was encouraged that Audrey at least ate a little of everything on her plate. Better than nothing, she supposed. It's pathetic, she thought, how a desperate parent can grab at the most meager thing. But she so missed the animated, talkative child that her daughter used to be. As much as she tried, she couldn't get a conversation up and running. Alice Tabor couldn't help but wonder what her daughter was thinking, but she knew that Audrey wouldn't tell her if she asked. She couldn't help but think of Gretchen. Would her beloved Audrey wind up in a hospital, too?

The last leg of the trip was the visit to Audrey's pediatrician, back toward the town center. Dr. Farrell had offices in Boston, Greenwood Springs, and another town not far down the road toward the city. He lived in Greenwood Springs, and it had been he who had suggested that the Tabors look for a home there.

Sitting in the corner chair of Dr. Farrell's examining room, Alice watched apprehensively as Audrey stepped onto the scale. The nurse continued to move the metal arrow further and further down the measuring bar, looking for a stopping place. From the back, Audrey looked like nothing more than a wrinkled heap of clothing — no bodily outline to be seen. Entering the weight on Audrey's chart, the nurse glanced quickly at Alice and left the room.

A few moments later Dr. Farrell entered the room, chart in hand.

"Well, Audrey, hop up on the table and let's take a look at that arm of yours," said the doctor.

As Audrey removed her shirt, both doctor and mother were alarmed at what they saw. Alice's breath caught in an audible gasp at the thin upper arms and protruding collarbones. Her eyes locked with those of Dr. Farrell. She looked at him as if to say, "I didn't know." She wondered ashamedly to herself, what kind of a mother she could be not to know? She was too overwhelmed to stop the tears.

Added to this was a very angry looking right arm — bloody sores from the upper arm to inside the elbow, with spots now blossoming on the forearm and down toward the wrist.

Dr. Farrell rolled his stool up close to Audrey, and gently began to speak.

"Audrey, something is bothering you. Something is making you very ill. You are too thin, and the cream I gave you earlier should have worked by now. Your skin is worse, not better."

"She's been eating a lot less lately, doctor," said Mrs. Tabor. "I guess less than I even realized." She looked tearfully at Audrey, who shifted her gaze to the floor.

Dr. Farrell looked thoughtfully at Audrey and slowly began to speak.

"Audrey, my dear, I have known you since you were a brand new baby. You were always one of my smartest, sweetest, happiest patients. You smiled and laughed and you played with other children in the waiting room. You have always been a joy to your mother and father. You were our rosy-cheeked girl."

He stopped briefly, took Audrey's hands in his, and continued in a warm, quiet voice.

"Now, I want you to hear this clearly. You are ten pounds under an acceptable weight for a healthy ten-year-old girl. Your once beautiful green eyes are dull, with deep shadows, and your face is sunken and pasty white. Your arms and legs are skinny and you haven't smiled once since you've arrived."

Audrey looked down into her lap, but Dr. Farrell demanded that she look into his eyes when he spoke.

"Look at me. You will become a very sick girl if you don't start eating a normal, healthy diet," the doctor advised.

Turning to Mrs. Tabor, who was visibly shaken, he continued, "I'm sure that whatever is causing the skin condition is causing the eating disorder, as well. When one improves the other will follow."

Audrey dressed while her pediatrician and mother conversed outside the examining room. Audrey couldn't hear the words, but she could hear the frantic tone in her mother's voice as she asked questions. Audrey wasn't sure what to think.

After receiving a new prescription for cream, the two left the medical building. Mrs. Tabor struggled to figure out how she could help her child, who was quite obviously suffering over something. She broke the awkward silence by offering — in her cheeriest voice — a trip to Davis's for two ice cream cones.

"I don't know, Mom. I had enough lunch. I shouldn't have ice cream, too."

"Audrey, I don't want to spoil this wonderful day by fighting, really. But what do you mean by 'I shouldn't have ice cream'? Who says you shouldn't be eating an ice cream cone?"

Audrey was remembering Hillary's comment that she was beginning to look even better than Lindsay in her bathing suit. And today proved that all her work was paying off. She couldn't ruin it by adding a big fattening ice cream to the sandwich and chips she'd nearly polished off earlier.

"I mean I'm not hungry. I had so much lunch that I'm full," answered Audrey quickly. "But you can go ahead and get one for yourself if you want, Mom."

Looking at her watch, Mrs. Tabor saw that it was already five o'clock and probably too late for an ice cream anyway. She began to think about the steak and baked potato dinner she had planned at home. It was Tom's favorite. (Matthew would miss his mashed potato highway, which was a good thing for the rest of the family.) So, instead of a stop at the ice cream parlor, Alice and her daughter headed for home.

When they arrived there, Tom Tabor shouted from Mattie's room, "I put the mail on the dining room table." He walked into the kitchen and continued, "Audrey, there's a letter for you, and Jessica left a message that I wrote down by the kitchen phone."

Audrey picked up both her letter and the telephone message and raced to her room, leaving the bags on the kitchen floor. The message said that the girls were going to meet on Saturday at eleven in the morning at Davis's Ice Cream, and then hang around town and maybe go back to Jessica's for a movie. It sounded to Audrey as if everything was O.K. She was happy and relieved. They really were good friends, after all.

The envelope addressed to her was small, the size of a little note card — the kind her mom wrote "get well's" and "thank you's" on. It was also the size of a party invitation. Her heart raced as she opened the envelope, anticipating the possibility of a birthday party. Jessica's? Lindsay's? What would she wear? On a small piece of unevenly cut white paper was a hand-printed note that said:

People are on to you.
You think you're a big deal, but you're not.
Better watch yourself, Audrey.

There was no signature and no return address. The words hurt her as surely as any physical blow. Why would anyone do this to her? And who *did* do it? She was frightened, as if a stranger were watching her, planning to do harm to her.

It took her breath away. Shaking badly from head to toe, she hid the letter under the papers in her desk drawer.

On Saturday morning, Audrey's mother took her to Davis's Ice Cream. They had arrived a full ten minutes early at Audrey's insistence. She was afraid of arriving late and missing her friends. She had been wide awake since four a.m., anyway, having tossed and turned throughout the long night, the letter weighing heavily on her mind.

The two sat in the car, watching eleven o'clock pass by, then eleven-fifteen, then finally eleven-thirty-five. Mrs. Tabor slowly pulled out of the parking lot, driving home a confused and disappointed Audrey.

CHAPTER

33

God does not intend us all to be rich, or powerful, or great,

but He does intend us all to be friends.

– Ralph Waldo Emerson

"Dad must have gotten the message wrong," said Audrey as she and her mother pulled into the driveway.

The whole incident made Audrey feel foolish — all the effort she went to in putting together just the right outfit; and all that insistence that her mother be out the door a good ten minutes earlier than necessary. For her fabulous day with the girls, Audrey had made sure on Friday evening that she manicured and polished her nails a dark pink. On Saturday morning she put up her hair in a French braid and tied it with an orchid ribbon to match her orchid shorts. She hid the dangly star earrings in her pocket, planning on switching them with the little studs that she was now wearing, the only style her mother would allow. Although her mother had finally consented to the piercing, she would not consent to any kind of earring that she deemed inappropriate or dangerous. Audrey knew it was wrong to be sneaky, especially as her mother had, after all allowed her to wear earrings, but her mother just didn't understand anything about fashion and friends and looking good. And now, here she was back home, all dressed with nothing to do.

"It's possible Dad could have misunderstood Jessica's message," answered Mrs. Tabor, as she opened the back door. "I guess, then, you never called Jessica back to confirm the message?"

"No, I figured I'd just show up. Do you think they might have meant next Saturday and Dad missed it?" asked Audrey.

"You know, honey, there's only one way to find out. Call Jessica and ask her."

"Maybe I'll just wait until I see her again, or something," said Audrey.

Leaning against the kitchen counter, Audrey's mother was silent for several seconds before speaking. "Audrey, are you embarrassed to call Jessica? You don't have to tell her you waited for them this morning. Just tell her you wanted to double check her message."

"Yeah, O.K., I guess I could do that," she agreed without much enthusiasm. It seemed like all the enthusiasm was taken right out of the whole day. She wished she could call another friend, but she had no other friends to call.

She started to make her way toward her room to change

into her old shorts and T-shirt. Just then the mail truck pulled up to the front walk as the phone began to ring.

Making for the phone, Mrs. Tabor shouted for Audrey to get the mail and put it on the kitchen counter. Mr. Tabor was unable to do either because he was out back playing ball with Matthew.

Audrey opened the front door, startling Mr. Adams, the neighborhood mailman, who was just about to place a thick wad of mail into the brass box nailed to the front of the house.

"Well, good morning, young lady!" chirped the ever-cheerful Mr. Adams.

"Hi, Mr. Adams," answered Audrey. "My mom said to get the mail."

The two conversed briefly about the beautiful weather and the fast approaching first day of school. Audrey took the stack of mail, and Mr. Adams gave his best to the family as he got back into his truck and drove to the next mailbox.

As Audrey walked through the front hall, absentmindedly riffling through the collection of letters and circulars, she stopped abruptly. There before her was a small envelope with no return address, similar to the one that came to her the day before. This time, she knew better than to anticipate any sort of invitation or party announcement. Her heart began to beat so that she could feel the pounding in her ears, and her stomach started twisting inside, making her feel sick. Letter in hand, she slowly climbed the stairs and entered her room, closing the door behind her. She tore open the flap and unfolded a piece of white paper, just like the one that was sent to her the last time. This time computer printed, the note said:

Nobody likes you, Audrey.
Losers have no friends.

And that was when the world fell apart for Audrey. Sinking down onto her bed and crumpling up like the piece of paper she had wadded in her fist, she began to cry. In her whole life, no one had ever hated Audrey. She smiled at everyone, was nice to people. She made friends easily. Kids always waved or nodded at her in the school hallways and playground. Lindsay had come right up to her in the cafeteria and introduced herself, and even Jessica had liked her right away. She didn't understand. Sometimes Hillary wasn't too nice; maybe it was Hillary. No, even Hillary wouldn't do this. Then Audrey started thinking about all the other kids in school that she had begun to ignore at the end of the year. Could it be one of them? Jessica did say that kids could be jealous of the most popular girls in school. But it wasn't fair. Audrey wasn't mean; she didn't deserve for this to happen. What was she going to do? How could she make it stop? What if her mother happened to open one of these letters one day?

She and Milly used to share their wishes and dreams. Gretchen shared her drawings and her innermost feelings. The sudden thought of these two friends made her feel even sadder and more alone. She had no one she could share her feelings with, not even Beth. She was just too embarrassed. And she didn't know why. This made her sob harder than she ever sobbed before. Between the morning's disappointment and this second horrible letter, Audrey felt like she was lost in a dark cave, with no hope of finding the way out on her own and no hope of rescue.

A sudden knock on the door and the sound of her mother's voice jolted Audrey out of her thoughts. Telling her mother in the brightest, calmest voice she could muster that she would be right there, Audrey hastily stuffed the note into its envelope and buried it in her desk drawer with the other letter. She quickly dried her eyes and sat herself at her desk, as if she were busy with a project. When she felt herself pulled together, she told her mother to come in.

"Oh, you haven't changed into your other clothes yet?"

Audrey told her mother that she had gotten a little busy. Alice Tabor looked at Audrey and thought she might have been crying, but decided to say nothing and see if her news would help the situation.

"That was Gretchen's mother on the phone," she said. "Gretchen is home now, and doing better. I think she misses you, Audrey. Mrs. Hart says her break-up with you made her think of those girls and the way they suddenly stopped wanting to be her friend. Anyway, I think it would be nice if you visited Gretchen or at least called her, don't you? You know, I always liked her and could never quite understand why you two became so angry with each other."

Before Audrey could respond, her mother said, "Hillary is one of the friends in your group. Did she used to be a friend of Gretchen's, too?"

"Yes, Hillary Wright. She was friendly with Gretchen when they were younger," answered Audrey with some embarrassment.

"I think they were best friends, according to Mrs. Hart," said her mother. "I guess," she continued, as if thinking out loud, "that I never made the connection. Hillary apparently ended the relationship badly and has been mean to Gretchen ever since. Did you know that?"

Scratching and rubbing her arm, Audrey responded, "Well, it's really her friends, Lindsay and Jessica, that I like. They're really nice to me. You know, Lindsay has such a nice family. You said so yourself. Hillary's not my favorite in the group, but..."

Mrs. Tabor gently interrupted Audrey's labored explanation. "I think you owe Gretchen a visit, don't you, Audrey?"

"Can you take me, Mom? I'd really like to see her."

Alice Tabor smiled warmly and said, "I sort of told Mrs. Hart that you'd be over, so I think she may be expecting you."

Audrey could have kissed her mother. She had so wanted to visit Gretchen but was afraid her old friend wouldn't let her in. And she figured that Alisha had probably taken her place anyway. Audrey's feeling that she was lost in a cave hadn't gone away, exactly; it was just that right now it didn't seem quite as dark. Was it a kind of happiness? Had she been so sad for so long that she forgot what happiness felt like? She knew one thing for sure: she wanted to see Gretchen more than anything.

CHAPTER

34

A faithful friend is a sturdy shelter.

He that has found one has found a treasure.

– Ecclesiastes 6:14

The walk down the little flagstone path to the front door of the pretty white ranch with green shutters seemed like the longest walk of Audrey's life. The Harts' home used to be a place of great warmth and happiness for Audrey. Now it just reminded her of things she had lost. The deep green door with its basket of silk flowers stood partly open, beckoning its visitors. As Audrey and her mom stood at its threshold, Audrey became nervous and fidgety. Gretchen's mother had told Audrey's mom that their fight made Gretchen feel sad. Was Mrs. Hart angry with Audrey now? Would Gretchen have anything to say to Audrey, or would she just sit there until she left? And would Gretchen be interested in anything that Audrey had to say?

When Mrs. Hart pulled open the door wide, most of

Audrey's fears vanished. The tall, slightly heavy-set woman gave both Audrey and her mom a broad smile and a warm hug.

"I'm so glad you came," said Irene Hart, as she ushered her guests into the living room. "This will give Gretchen such a lift. Audrey, we've missed you. It's nice to see you again."

The Tabors followed Mrs. Hart through the house and into the family room. Gretchen was sitting at the round table by the window, playing a game of scrabble with Alisha Krantz. The girls were talking quietly and smiling broadly. It looked to Audrey like they were having a great time and didn't need her to spoil things. She figured Alisha probably didn't like her anyway because of her friends. Getting a little closer, she noticed that Gretchen had put on some weight in her cheeks and around her middle. A bit overweight to begin with, Audrey thought that Gretchen really couldn't afford to put on any more pounds. Suddenly she caught herself — was she wrong to think this way? Was she behaving like Lindsay and the girls? Audrey didn't seem to know anymore.

"Dear," said Mrs. Hart tenderly, "you have some more company."

Gretchen and Alisha turned and looked up from their game. Audrey stood stock-still, awaiting Gretchen's reaction. After waiting a second or two for recognition, Gretchen's face, much like her mother's, erupted in a bright, happy smile. It was a wide smile that sat sweetly between two full, dimpled cheeks and was punctuated by the clearest of blue eyes. There was no mistaking Gretchen's happiness at seeing Audrey. Both girls met in the middle of the room. Audrey paused for just a moment, unsure of what to do, but then Gretchen threw an arm around Audrey's shoulders and led her to the sofa.

Getting up from her chair, Alisha said, "Well, I guess I'll leave now and let you guys visit."

Audrey wondered if Alisha was trying to be helpful, or if she was leaving because she didn't like her.

Gretchen quickly insisted, "No, no, Alisha, please stay. We can all sit and talk, O.K.? Please?"

After a moment, Alisha nodded at the two girls, both now seated on the sofa. Although she sat herself down in the chair that faced them, she appeared to be a bit uncomfortable. Adjusting and readjusting her thick glasses and pulling at her fingers, Alisha had all the body language of someone waiting for bad news. Audrey looked away, and focused her attention on Gretchen.

Audrey started, "I'm sorry I didn't get to see you sooner, but my mom said you weren't ready for visitors."

"Yeah," answered Gretchen, "I was a real mess for a while." She looked to Alisha, who nodded in agreement.

It was apparent to Audrey that Alisha had indeed become a good friend. She was glad for Gretchen and sad for herself.

"Gretchen, is it all right if I ask you what happened? How

did you wind up in the hospital? I feel so bad," said Audrey softly, and with great concern.

Gretchen looked down into her lap as she twisted a lock of her hair. It seemed forever to Audrey before Gretchen spoke. Audrey was beginning to feel as if maybe she shouldn't have asked the question.

"I guess I didn't like anything anymore," Gretchen began thoughtfully. "My mom would ask if I wanted to go shopping or see a movie and I would scream at her. I yelled at my brothers. I tore up a lot of my drawings, and couldn't stop crying. Eating wasn't making me feel better anymore. And then I started to cut my arm a little bit, and that made me feel better."

"What do you mean, 'cut your arm,' Gretchen?" Picturing knives and scissors and blood, Audrey's eyes took on a look of horror and confusion.

"See?" whispered Gretchen, holding out her left arm.

Tiny scars, some pink, some white, made a bizarre pattern on the inside of her forearm.

"My mom said she found me in my room and I was all messed up. I guess my arm was bleeding, but I don't really remember all of it. Anyway, that's when I went to the hospital."

Audrey felt as though the air had left her body, and then she began to cry. Gretchen reached out for Audrey's hand and said gently, "Don't cry, Audrey. I'm sorry I said I never wanted to see you again. I didn't really mean it. I shouldn't tell you who you can be friendly with. It's none of my business."

Audrey couldn't believe that Gretchen was apologizing to her — after all Gretchen had been through, after all Audrey had done. And the tears kept rolling slowly down her face.

"Anyway," continued Gretchen, "you may have noticed that I'm not the thinnest person in the world. My whole family is kind of chubby. And then when I'm bored or unhappy, I eat. After we stopped hanging out, I guess I started eating too much, and then I got really depressed when I had to get bigger clothes, so I kept on eating, right Lish?"

Alisha spoke so quietly that Audrey had to lean toward her to pick up everything she said. "I have the same problem — as if that's a big surprise to everyone, right?" she laughed sarcastically. "I know that kids make fun of me because of the way I look. It makes me feel bad, sometimes mad. My mom has spent thousands on doctors, diets, therapists — she tried everything to get me to lose weight. We live near Jessica Morton, and I have to ride the school bus with her every day, so I know what Gretchen's going through." Alisha and Gretchen smiled warmly at each other.

Gretchen responded, "Alisha's a great friend." When she saw Audrey smile weakly, and look down at her hands, she added, "She's a good person. Just like you, Audrey."

At those words of kindness, a feeling came up in Audrey from very deep down. It moved up through the middle of her, into the heart of her, and overcame her. The anger and sadness that had been stuffed down inside her for so long came up and spilled over in a torrent of tears. Head down and shoulders shaking, Audrey was embraced lovingly by her friend, who was now crying, too. Alisha motioned a silent goodbye to Gretchen, and she nodded in return.

Alarmed at the sound of gut-wrenching sobbing, both Mrs. Tabor and Mrs. Hart ran to the family room, peering carefully around the doorframe to see what was going on. At the sight of both girls embracing in tears, both mothers broke down, and the Hart household was filled to the brim with crying women.

For the remainder of the day, Gretchen and Audrey spoke with ease. Audrey had forgotten how good it felt to have someone she could really speak to, who could actually understand her spirit, the real Audrey. She talked about her summer at the pool, and what it was like to spend time on the edge of these spoiled girls' lives. She described the way Hillary tried to do the same, hiding herself behind fancy clothes and imitating the mean girls she thought were so cool. In particular, she appologized to Gretchen about ever having become friendly with Hillary, a cruel, mean girl who'd hurt her friend so deeply. Audrey was hurt, too, but she'd learned how bad if felt to hurt someone else, someone who was your true friend.

Audrey could not yet tell her friend, however, about the way she'd hidden the clothes the girls bought her, or how she'd sneaked into school the things that she wasn't allowed to wear.

And she couldn't tell her about the mean notes she had hidden in her desk drawer; not today. But her heart was lighter for the time she was spending with Gretchen.

Gretchen listened with the open heart of a friend. There were things that Gretchen had learned and needed to share, as well, and she would, in time. For now, however, Gretchen said enough so that Audrey could begin to feel how frightened she had been. With just that inkling of what Gretchen had been through, Audrey found herself flooded with gratitude that Gretchen was home, that she was here. And she knew that she would treasure Gretchen, because Gretchen was a true friend.

The afternoon had passed its prime, and at her mother's insistence, Audrey reluctantly stood up to leave. As Gretchen hugged her lost and found friend, she said suddenly, "Hey, Audrey, I may be fat and ugly, but you're not looking so good, either! You look thin and raggedy, and tired. And what's that stuff on your arms? It looks like you've been rolling around in poison ivy."

Audrey smiled. "You sound just like my mother, Gretchen!"

But Audrey didn't mind at all. In fact, it sounded just right to her.

"I haven't been feeling so good, Gretch, but I think I'm starting to feel better now."

CHAPTER
35

I have perceived that to be with those I like is enough.

– *Walt Whitman*

The summer ran out of days and slowly disappeared, as summers always do. The leaves on the trees had moved through the season, from a newborn yellow to a wise old deep green, gradually nearing the end of their lushness. Rolling waves still met the hot sand, and blue pool water still sparkled under the bright sun. But the children were mostly gone now to other places. Backpacks replaced towels; sweaters were displayed in department stores where tank tops and bathing suits used to be. Fall library hours and bus schedules were now listed in the *Greenwood Springs Town Crier*; no more day camp notices appeared. The days were still hot, but now they began and ended with an unmistakable crispness. It was September.

On the phone, Jessica had assured Audrey that the message she had left with Audrey's dad was, indeed, misunderstood —

that the plans were for a later Saturday. But, as it turned out, the day had to be put on hold due to difficulty in scheduling. She told Audrey that she felt awful about her having waited for nothing. Audrey felt better. Afterwards they discussed the first day of school, which was a week away on the following Wednesday, two days after Labor Day.

Audrey was nervous about starting sixth grade, but excited about wearing one of the beautiful new outfits that she and her mother had picked out at the mall. She had her pencils, pens, and other classroom tools ready in her new bright blue zippered bag. It was weird to Audrey how, just a few weeks ago, she couldn't think of anything but swimming and now could barely remember the excitement she felt at the first sight of the country club pool.

And then this last week of vacation passed nearly without notice. Lindsay and her family went to Cape Cod, so Audrey spent the week in the school's day camp program. Lindsay's mom had also called Mrs. Tabor to say that, since the girls were in the sixth grade, she wanted Lindsay to spend more time on her studies after school and it wouldn't be convenient for Audrey to come home after school. This meant Audrey would be back in the after school program, but in some ways Audrey was relieved. She did ask her mom if she could just come home alone since she was getting older, but Mrs. Tabor was not quite ready for that.

Then suddenly The First Day of School came, and children were meeting, as ever, at bus stops, in corridors, and in new classroom doorways. This year, Gretchen was not in Audrey's homeroom class, but neither was Lindsay. Instead, Audrey and Jessica were in Mrs. Reed's class, and Gretchen and Lindsay were in Miss Elmore's. Audrey was relieved that she didn't have Miss Elmore for math; she'd heard she was hard. Hillary was in Brianna's class, which must have made the two of them very happy, since they still seemed inseparable.

At the first recess on that Wednesday, the Style Girls reclaimed their hill, and they all stood around admiring each other's looks and clothing. Jessica had spent the last week of vacation shopping for clothes with her mom in New York City, and was posing like a fashion model for her friends. Everyone seemed to be in a great mood, and Audrey spent the time complimenting the other girls on their clothes, earrings, and hair clips, hoping they had forgotten the bad feelings from the end of the summer. Somehow, however, her heart wasn't really in it.

New books and new teachers made the beginning of every school year confusing, but Audrey managed to get through the first few weeks as well as could be expected, and certainly better than when she'd been "the new girl from Boston." Disregarding the Style Girls' advice, she began smiling and nodding at other students as they passed her in the hallways or worked beside her in social studies. Many, still hurt from her previous attitude, did not respond. But she accepted that and was patient. And now, when she and

Gretchen passed in the halls, they always smiled and waved and, when possible, stopped briefly to chat. Audrey continued to spend recess and lunchtime with the group, but Gretchen wasn't angry anymore. Audrey even stopped by often to chat with Gretchen and Alisha before joining her other friends across the lunchroom. Audrey's new behavior did not go unnoticed by the Style Girls. Sometimes she caught Hillary and Jessica staring at her and whispering to each other — or maybe Audrey was just imagining something that really had nothing to do with her.

"Everybody, this is Tyra DeAngelo," announced Hillary one day at lunch.

Standing before the group was a tall, tanned, dark-eyed girl with the most beautiful dark brown-nearly-black silky hair Audrey had ever seen. Looking around, she could tell that the rest of the group was pretty impressed with her, as well. Tyra was wearing a very short blue pleated skirt (much shorter than would ever in a million years be allowed at Audrey's house), a cropped pink T-shirt and blue sandals. She wore jewelry everywhere: bracelets, earrings, a pendant made of some bright, beautiful stone. So this was the girl that Hillary had spoken about.

Jessica invited her to sit down and introduced all the girls at the table. When she got to Audrey, she said, "Tyra, this is Audrey, who still seems to be having a little trouble following the group rules, don't you, Aud?"

Audrey was shaken by the remark, which came out of the blue.

"Huh?" she answered, as she held her fork in mid-air, spaghetti falling off the side.

Hillary was more than happy to offer an explanation.

"You'll smile at any old nobody, won't you, Audrey? And, O-M-G, loser-city over there," she drawled snidely, jerking her head in the direction of Gretchen and Alisha's table and forming an "L" on her forehead with her thumb and index finger. "What are the chances that by Christmas your pals, the Blimp Twins, might just explode?"

Brianna was beside herself in hysterics, leaning on Hillary's arm. Even Tyra joined in by adding an unkind remark and a sly smile. And Lindsay suppressed a giggle behind her napkin.

Audrey stood up and gathered her lunch tray and plastics. Jessica, Hillary, Brianna, and the new recruit were still laughing, but Lindsay spoke.

"Audrey, we're only kidding. You don't have to leave."

Audrey shook with anger and nervousness at what she was about to say, but she said it because it needed to be said. "No, Lindsay, I don't think you're ever really kidding about anything, even though you always say you are. I think you're all pretty nasty. I think you and your friends mean what you say all the time. You're even mean to each other. What kind of friends are you, anyway?"

Looking up, Jessica responded, "You've got a real nerve, talking to Lindsay that way, Audrey, after everything she's done for you."

"I appreciate staying at Lindsay's and all the nice stuff she bought me. But it still doesn't make it all right to hurt people's feelings. And why don't you let Lindsay speak for herself for a change?"

The group caught its collective breath in shock at Audrey's comment.

Then Brianna broke the silence. "Did you have a nice summer, Audrey?" she asked, with a smirk on her face. She seemed happy to be leading the assault. "Staying for free at a fancy country club that you could never afford, and you know it."

"Yeah, and I guess it was O.K. for you to just keep accepting all the clothes and things we bought you, huh?" added Hillary.

Answered Audrey quickly, "If you call working as a slave being a free guest. Did I ever tell you how much I hated getting food and finding beach balls for everyone? And you know what? I'll be happy to put all the stuff you bought me in a big trash bag and return it to everyone. I don't want to wear any of it anymore."

"You ought to think twice about that, Miss Big Deal Loser," sneered Hillary, "because those rags your mommy bought you are totally nowhere. Oh my God, where *do* you people shop, anyway?"

"Gretchen was right about you, Hillary," said Audrey. "You are the meanest person in school, maybe even in town, and that makes you the ugliest. It doesn't matter what you wear or where you shop. I can't believe I ever wasted my time with you. You call everyone a loser, but you're the loser, Hillary, and Gretchen was smart enough to know it!"

"And my mother was right about you, Audrey!" sneered Lindsay, eyes narrowed in anger.

"What's that supposed to mean?" said Audrey.

"She warned me not to hang out with girls like you, from the wrong families. And your family has no education and no money!"

Hillary was about to say something, but Audrey didn't wait to hear it. As she abruptly turned to go, she stopped briefly and said to Tyra so that everyone could hear, "Hey, good luck with the Style Girls, Tyra. Look around and make sure you really want to fit in."

At that moment, the bell rang for recess. Walking away toward the trash barrel, Audrey heard the words "loser" and "creep" accompanied by more sickening laughter. This time she wasn't trying to tell herself that it was just her imagination.

Lindsay was one of the first students who left the cafeteria. Spotting Audrey, she caught up with her. Lindsay's sudden appearance caught Audrey's breath, and their eyes locked for what seemed like an eternity.

Deliberately and quietly Lindsay whispered, "I thought you were my friend, Audrey."

"I was," Audrey replied.

With that, Lindsay turned and walked away. Audrey's eyes followed her long strides down the corridor – perfect little outfit, perfect blonde ponytail. The cafeteria students began filling up more and more of the hallway, and soon all she could see was that blonde ponytail bobbing and bouncing up and down and side to side. Just before Audrey turned to join Gretchen, she noticed Lindsay's hand adjusting that bit of blonde perfection as she faded out of sight.

Audrey caught up with Gretchen. As they walked, arm in arm to the schoolyard, it suddenly occurred to Audrey that back in the cafeteria, Hillary had called her a "big deal loser." "Big deal" were the same words printed on the letter she had received.

And, as she thought more about it, she figured that Jessica probably really did leave that phone message — exactly the way her dad had written it.

CHAPTER

36

What do we live for,

if it is not to make life less difficult to others?

– George Eliot

During afternoon recess, Gretchen invited a shaken Audrey to resume their old after school arrangement in the cafeteria Kids' Klub. It was true that Audrey was upset about the words that had been exchanged during lunch. But it was also true that she was enjoying an unexpected feeling of calm. Something had changed for her, and it was good. In addition, both girls were very pleased and excited about their plans to spend afternoons together again. They knew that they had much to discuss.

Returning to her homeroom after language lab, Audrey found a piece of folded paper sticking out from under her notebook. Sliding casually into her seat, she quickly removed and unfolded the note. The penmanship looked hurried and careless, the thin black marker smudged and uneven. It said:

*You're just a sad joke
and
everyone hates you.*

Audrey folded the note in fourths and, trying to appear casual, placed it in the back pocket of her jeans. She remained distracted for the last hour of school, scanning the class every few minutes for possible suspects. Sometimes her eyes would fix on Jessica, wondering what role she might be playing in all of this. At times the two girls would accidentally lock eyes and then quickly look away. Replaying the note's mean words over and over in her head, Audrey missed most of her social studies lesson on China and failed to notice that the next chapter of reading was assigned. Audrey's distracted behavior worsened through the last class of the day. Music was a blur, lost in a haze of guilt and self doubt.

Audrey wandered into the hallway at the closing bell and collected the wrong blue backpack. Realizing her mistake, she turned to exchange it for her own. Standing at the coat hook was a very confused Harriet Pratt, looking for the blue backpack that Audrey was wearing. Audrey handed her classmate her backpack, staring vacantly, while Harriet laughed, commenting that they needed to put special key chains on their packs so that they could tell them apart from now on. Audrey didn't hear her.

Everyone hates you. Over and over again these frightening words hammered in her head. One inside voice said that it wasn't true, while the other voice told her maybe it was. Maybe Milly hated her. She should. Audrey didn't call her anymore. Maybe she deserved that note.

As the after-school crowd moved Audrey toward the cafeteria, more thoughts bombarded her. Maybe she was a just a joke. After what she did to Gretchen maybe she didn't deserve to have her as a friend. Maybe nobody should be her friend. Ever.

Passing Lindsay, who completely ignored her, along the way, Audrey looked up to see Gretchen standing and waving wildly at her from the table in the far corner of the room.

"Hey, Audrey," said Gretchen as Audrey approached her table. "Where are you? Are you O K ?"

Gretchen looked at her friend, whose hollow eyes seemed to be looking at nothing. She placed her hand on Audrey's shoulder and whispered, "Audrey, What's wrong?"

Audrey locked eyes with Gretchen and, trying very hard not to cry, murmured softly, "Gretchen, do you like me?"

"You know I like you, Audrey. You're my friend," she answered with a bright, warm smile. "What's this all about?"

She took a breath and began to tell Gretchen all about the things that had been going on since their friendship was interrupted.

The conversation that began in the cafeteria continued until Mrs. Tabor appeared at the door to pick up Audrey. That day, as it happened, Mrs. Hart was a little later than usual and arrived at almost exactly the same moment to pick up Gretchen. It had been a long afternoon, but it didn't seem so to the girls. Audrey told Gretchen about the beautiful homes and gigantic T.V. and the fancy country club and pool. She also described her job as the group gofer, and all the times she had to get drinks and snacks and fish out sandals that "accidentally" fell into the pool. She told Gretchen about the way Lindsay didn't like to share her recipes and about the fights the girls would have with each other. She told her, ashamedly, about all the clothes and extra things she'd allowed the girls to buy her, and about the way she'd lied to her mother and sneaked her new things into school. She went on to describe the day that no one showed up at the ice cream stand. And when Audrey slowly pulled out the note from her pocket, Gretchen listened in disbelief about the other mean messages that were hidden in Audrey's desk. Gretchen made Audrey promise to show them to her and not to throw them away.

When Audrey actually listened to the words as she spoke them for the first time, it all sounded so terrible. She wondered how she could not have noticed how awful her life had become since joining the Style Girls. As Gretchen clutched her hand, Audrey wondered how she could have turned her back on a friend who really cared about her for a bunch of nasty nobodies. And suddenly, she remembered Beth's warning to stay away from the "mean girls." Why hadn't she listened?

Gretchen, in turn, quietly described her battle with depression, and how one day she threw her mother's favorite bowl against the wall, shattering it to pieces. She spoke about how her behavior had affected her mother, father, and brothers, and how sad and guilty it made her feel, and how the sadder and guiltier she felt, the worse her behavior became. She told her that she couldn't help herself, that nothing she did was right, and that she was terrified, and lost, and — trapped — inside her own mind. She described how the nurses at the hospital were kind to her, and how her doctor helped her look for the reasons behind her illness. And then she showed Audrey the pictures she had been drawing. Audrey studied her friend's remarkable sketches — some of girls deep in thought, or crying alone, or sharing in friendship, and some of lonely landscapes and deep snowy woods. They told a painful story of sadness and hope and great strength. For Audrey, it brought to mind the beautiful drawing that Gretchen had so lovingly given to her. And then she remembered Milly's picture of the two girls on the bench.

The talk made Audrey feel better, but later in the day the doubts crept back into her head. And the words. The words the words the words...

That evening her dad came home from work earlier than usual, always a happy occurrence. Mattie was at his friend Adam's house for dinner — one less vegetable turnpike.

And Audrey's mom made meatloaf with Audrey's favorite sweet and sour sauce. But tonight it was like none of this was happening.

"...so I finished the report, made Phil happy, and here I am! Home early and all yours. Lucky you!" smiled Tom Tabor as he took his first forkful of meatloaf.

"Oh, honey, I'm so glad," answered Alice. She sat down to join the family at the table. "Maybe later we'll have hot fudge sundaes for dessert. I bought some ice cream from Davis's."

"Audrey," said her dad, "will you please pass the salt?"

Audrey sat as still as petrified wood, not eating a bit of food, eyes fixed on the wall.

Mr. Tabor continued, "The salt? Audrey? Honey?"

Mrs. Tabor noticed the scenario and quikly shook Audrey's shoulder. "Are you feeling ill, honey?"

Mr. and Mrs. Tabor glanced quickly at each other. She put down her fork and he stopped buttering his bread.

"Audrey," said her mother, "Don't do this. You know what the doctor told you. You need to eat. You're thin enough."

"Thin enough?" exclaimed her father angrily. "I'd say too damned thin, young lady!"

"Tom, please! Your language!" admonished Alice.

"Oh, my language? Really? Is that what we're concerned about here? Our daughter is wasting away for God's sake! Look at her!" With that Tom Tabor threw down his napkin, nearly tipped over his chair, and stormed into the living room.

"Audrey," said Alice, "you are scaring your dad and me. This is one of your favorite foods. Please try and eat a little. You will get very, very sick and have to go to a hospital."

Everyone hates you! Hates you! Hates you! The words, the words in her head. "No, no! It's not true!" she yelled.

"Oh, it's true, all right. You'll go to a hospital, Audrey!" her mother yelled in a panic.

Startled, Audrey looked up. "What? No, it's not that. I mean, I just don't feel so good Mom," she replied haltingly. "My stomach hurts."

Mrs. Tabor felt her head for sign of fever; there was none. Audrey was excused and her mother slumped defeatedly in her chair. A perfectly wonderful dinner became leftovers for another night. What followed was an unpleasant and difficult evening. Mattie returned and soon was tucked into bed. Audrey sat in a corner of the family room with a book that she only pretended to read. And Tom and Alice barely said a half dozen words to each other while the T.V. droned.

CHAPTER

37

Friendship with the man of specious airs;

friendship with the insinuatingly soft;

and friendship with the glib-tongued;

These are injurious.

– Confucius

After lying awake nearly the whole night, Audrey arose at 5:30 a.m. Staring without interest at her closet, she chose jeans and some nondescript top. Not wanting to awaken the household and cause her family to ask why she was up so early, she tiptoed carefully to her chair and waited until she heard sounds of life in the house. It seemed like forever, but finally seven o'clock came, and drawers slammed opened and shut and blinds banged against window frames.

At seven twenty-five, Audrey made her way to the kitchen. As she shook Cheerios into a bowl, her dad joined her. Kissing her on the head he spoke.

"You know how much we all love you Audrey. Both your mom and I want you to be the healthy happy girl you have always been."

"I know, Dad." She poured her milk over the cereal and began eating at the counter.

"Dad?" she said.

"What, honey?"

"Nothing."

"Is there something you want to say, Audrey? You know your old dad. I'm all ears." He made a goofy face and pulled on his ears. Audrey smiled in spite of herself.

"I was just wondering, Dad. What was it like when you went to school?"

Mr. Tabor was formulating a reply to his daughter's surprising question when suddenly a half-dressed Mattie ran headlong into the kitchen. He was followed promptly by his clearly aggravated mother who was holding a pair of blue pants. Alice grabbed her squealing son and turned to see her daughter eating a bowl of cereal.

"Oh, good morning, Audrey. Are you feeling better? I'm glad you're having breakfast."

"Mom?" asked Audrey, "Can Dad drive me to school today? The bus sometimes gets noisy."

Tom smiled and nodded and Alice agreed. Audrey did not make this request often and her mother wondered if this had anything to do with the incident at last night's dinner table. But right now she needed to get a very stubborn little boy dressed.

It was a nice, peaceful fifteen-minute ride with her

dad, and Audrey was relieved not to be on the school bus this morning. She was watching the beautifully colored trees go by when her father suddenly broke the silence.

"So, what was it like when I went to school? You mean when I was your age?"

Audrey couldn't believe he remembered the question.

"Yeah, I mean, you know, like with friends and stuff."

"Hmm. Well, I had a couple of good pals. We fooled around in class sometimes. You didn't hear that!" he grinned.

"We hung out, played a little pick-up football, ate pizza. You know, what kids do."

"I wish I was a boy and that's all we did."

"I thought you liked to shoot baskets with Gretchen, and didn't you used to have pizza and go to the movies with Milly? What's the difference?"

And then, without realizing it, Audrey was at the school drop-off door. She grabbed her things and kissed her dad. She opened the car door, but before flying out she turned and said, "I love you, Dad."

Throughout her school day, through math and gym and social studies, the same question pounded her brain: Who? Who wrote those things? Who would do that to me? Lunchtime brought sneers from Jessica. Hillary bumped into Audrey accidentally-on-purpose when they were changing classes. And she did it again later in the day. Somehow she was able to survive the school day, but was too exhausted to enjoy even Gretchen's after-school company.

When Audrey returned home that evening, she thought about all the people she loved. She thought about what her dad had said in the car. She thought about the way she felt when she was with Gretchen and the way she felt when she was with the other girls. And then she knew what she had to do.

Slamming her closet door open against its adjacent wall, she crawled on her hands and knees, roughly yanking out the pants, skirts, and tops that were lying hidden in places where she alone could find them. She then stood up, snatching additional garments from their plastic hangers. The hangers were thrown with a clatter to the closet floor, while the clothing, some of it now ripped, was dumped onto her bedroom rug. Stomping harshly over the heap of expensive gifts and kicking a few out of her way, Audrey proceeded to rummage through her top bureau drawers, hurling assorted earrings, bracelets, and hair clips in the direction of the discarded mess. Furiously slamming drawers shut and wrenching out others, she moved on to her stash of fashion and gossip magazines. Turned out of their upended plastic storage container, her sole summer reading material hit the floor hard, leaving some covers twisted, some torn. The noisy rampage continued with drawers being pulled out and turned over. Through it all, Audrey made sure she saved the letters, as Gretchen had requested.

In the midst of all the tossing and slamming, Audrey stopped. Lying in the debris was the silver heart bracelet from her beloved aunt and uncle, broken by Jessica and then hidden away by Audrey.

And then she spotted it. Peeking out from under a pile of wrinkled papers was a picture frame. Audrey tugged on the corner, as it slowly revealed itself. There they were — the two little girls still sitting side by side on their bench proclaiming to be "Friends Forever." The glass was deeply cracked.

The racket couldn't help but catch the attention of the family. So immersed was Audrey in her mission that she did not see her mother standing at her bedroom door. Angrily grasping Audrey' polka dot mini-skirt and long silver earrings, Mrs. Tabor was fully prepared to initiate a confrontation about these items. However, her anger quickly turned to disbelief at the sight of her daughter's shockingly disastrous room. The bedroom looked like a landfill — strewn, fragmented, layered, and torn — a frenzied heap of nameless, unwanted things. A ripped magazine cover here, the sleeve of a pink shirt there, the gleam of something silver peeking our from under something blue. Upturned drawers and plastic boxes and emptied shelves.

But most startling and most frightening to Audrey's mother was the sight of her precious child sitting among the ruins, looking so very angry and so very small.

Forgetting all but the scene before her, Mrs. Tabor dropped the skirt and silver earrings she had been holding.

They slipped silently through her fingers, taking their place among the other discarded items.

"Audrey?" she murmured gently.

Startled at the sound of her mother's voice, Audrey raised her head. As she looked into her mother's frightened eyes, she wondered how she would explain all this. What could she say? Where do you begin when you don't even know yourself where the beginning is?

And then suddenly the strangest thing happened.

She said, simply, "Mommy."

The word startled Audrey's mother who hadn't heard her daughter call her "Mommy" in a long time. But it startled Audrey even more.

Audrey began to cry deeply and unrestrainedly.

"Mommy," choked Audrey, "I'm sorry."

Mrs. Tabor walked into the room, dropped to her knees, and clutched her little girl. It was in this pile of misery that Audrey told her mother about her mean friends and about the hair clips, the earrings, and fancy outfits. She talked about the mocha cake and the pool. She even admitted to hiding her new clothes in her backpack and changing in school. And the letters — oh those awful letters. But the hardest thing that she ever had to do in her whole life was to admit to her mother how she betrayed her friend, Gretchen, just so she could be with the popular girls.

Audrey's red cheeks were lined in salty rivulets of tears.

Her swollen eyes were so filled with water she could barely see. Her hands lay limp beside her as her head hung low.

Mrs. Tabor, who was weeping too, put Audrey's wet face in her hands and lifted it slowly to meet her own.

Still gasping out uncontrolled sobs, Audrey whispered, "I'm sorry, Mom."

"No, sweetheart. I'm sorry. I am so sorry that I didn't realize what was going on. I knew you weren't happy, but I should have tried harder to help you. I wasn't a good mother when you needed me to be."

"You mean you're not mad at me?" asked Audrey.

Mrs Tabor caught her breath, and then exhaled gradually.

"Audrey," she replied slowly and thoughtfully, "I think that a lot of the decisions you've made throughout this whole ordeal were not good ones. But you realize that now. Sometimes we have to learn the hard way about how to be good people, how to be good friends."

Audrey's mother paused thoughtfully, and then continued.

"Audrey, those awful notes you talked about — those were written by angry and unhappy people. Angry, unhappy people can become mean and they make up mean things just to hurt others. You know in your heart that these things they wrote are all lies."

Audrey nodded silently.

Mrs. Tabor continued, holding her daughter's hands in

her own. "You have family and friends who love you because you are a good person. That means everything, and these letters mean nothing. They're trash, not worth the paper they're printed on. The best thing we can do when we receive things like these is ignore them, tear them up."

Mrs. Tabor paused and smiled. "And from the contents of this room, I think you probably know who wrote them."

Audrey thought that she couldn't love anybody as much as she loved her mother at that moment. And then mother and daughter sat on the floor and hugged and hugged for a blissfully long time.

The smile on Alice Tabor's face was radiant. "Honey, I'm so proud of you today for having the courage to tell me all of this. I can't even begin to imagine how difficult it must have been for you. I love you, Audrey."

Audrey went on to tell her mother about wanting to throw the gifts in a trash bag and return them to the girls. She related the cafeteria conversation. Mrs. Tabor suggested that they pack the gifts nicely in boxes, and said that she would help Audrey return them.

"And Mom," added Audrey, "do you think Milly will ever talk to me again? I haven't called her and I missed her birthday."

"Well, honey," answered her mother, "all you can do is call her and be honest with her like you were with me. You owe her that."

The following Saturday Audrey called Milly. A long heartfelt confession and tearful apology lifted the final weight.

CHAPTER

38

True friends are like diamonds, precious and rare;
False ones, like autumn leaves, found everywhere.

– Anonymous

Jack o lanterns again took their annual places of honor on front steps, porches, and in livingroom windows. The Tabors' pumpkin sat on the front landing, waiting to be carved. Pots of late-summer blue asters gave way to bright yellow, dark red and orange chrysanthemums nestled alongside the pumpkins on display. On any given street, wanderers could find little white cloth ghosts hanging from tree branches and pretend cobwebs strung across doorways. The sight was marred by the occasional smashed pumpkin, usually lying sadly in the road. Summer-green lawns now lay faded under a crunchy coverlet of orange and brown. The mean notes that had been coming to Audrey seemed to dry up like the autumn leaves and finally stopped arriving.

Days were cool and fresh and as crisp as the leaves that

gave the season its name. Sometimes the remembrance of summer would return for a little while, but fall was settling in for the long haul. Families were renting spooky movies on the weekends and parents were taking their children on hayrides. Mulled cider had replaced iced tea, and apple pies made from apples bought or picked at local orchards were cooling on kitchen counters. Halloween was still two weeks away, but the good citizens of Greenwood Springs would never think of denying their children or themselves the full anticipation of a major holiday.

Gretchen, Audrey, Milly, Alisha, and Beth were sitting at the Tabors' kitchen table, with posterboard, markers, glue, and various other materials spread out before them. Some of the supplies had fallen to the floor. Gretchen had volunteered her friends' services in the creation of a poster for the upcoming Halloween party at the Elks' Hall. The best poster would win a prize. The girls, not as artistic as Gretchen, weren't sure they could be helpful, but they did their best. Milly was blown away by Gretchen's drawings and felt that she was in the presence of a true genius. It made Gretchen laugh.

Amidst the mess sat Mattie, playing contentedly at Audrey's feet. His trucks had lately been put aside for an impressive set of plastic dinosaurs whose long names he had taken to reciting to Audrey — frequently.

This had been a special day, thanks to Audrey's mother. Because Audrey's eleventh birthday had fallen in the previous week and because she had missed Milly's birthday the previous April, her mom thought that perhaps a joint celebration in honor of their friendship would be the perfect thing. And, of course, no party would be complete without Gretchen and Beth. Beth was happy to be celebrating her favorite cousin's birthday. She was relieved to see her back with her friends, and pleased to meet her new one. And it had not gone unnoticed by Mrs. Tabor that Milly was a very special child in her ability to forgive and understand.

Over the past few weeks, Audrey was beginning to heal. Her face was fuller and less pale, and her itching seemed to have stopped. Certainly, if the grilled cheese and tomato sandwiches she and Milly had wolfed down the day before were any indication, things were greatly improving. Listening to the group of jabbering girls made Mrs. Tabor suddenly realize how long it had been since the sound of female friendship had filled her home.

"What are you going to be this year, Gretchen?" asked Milly as she placed a skeleton cutout on the board.

"I was thinking, maybe a nurse, and I could use a black medicine bag for candy. I'm still working on the idea," said Gretchen.

Audrey rubbed a glue stick across the middle of the posterboard and threw orange and black glitter over it. She asked, "How about you, Mil? What will you be?"

"My mom says I should be a tornado because my

room always looks like it was hit by one!" answered Milly. Everyone giggled.

"Well," said Audrey, "maybe I'll be a superhero, maybe Catwoman."

"I'm gonna be Tyrannosaurus Rex," added Mattie as he roared and moved his plastic prehistoric pieces under the table.

"That sounds like a good idea, Mattie," smiled his sister, and a round of good natured laughter filled the room.

The dark orange poster displayed a pumpkin-headed skeleton throwing magic glitter and ghosts and goblins from a hat. (Gretchen had done most of the drawing.) The title said, "Halloween Party! All Creatures Are Welcome!" in words that were made up of tiny tile-like mosaics.

There was nothing extraordinary about the title — until you looked very closely. Each little mosaic piece was made from a torn bit of Audrey's mean notes.

Glued down until not a fragment was left.

The brilliant reds and golds of autumn were fading fast to a dull, brittle brown. And soon, the washed out world would be still and hard and white, waiting patiently for earth's garden to return.

But Audrey's garden was blooming. Even better than a garden of flowers, hers was filled to the brim with good friends.

And all the colors were bright and true.

Friends are like flowers.
Once planted they make our life a garden.

—Anonymous

Leslie Koresky

AUTHOR'S NOTE

You don't meet many young Audreys these days. It is a name more associated with a previous era. So then, you might ask why I chose "Audrey" for the name of my heroine.

I named Audrey after Audrey Hepburn, a famous movie star (and one of my favorites) who lived many years ago. Audrey Hepburn's renowned grace, beauty, and strong connection with her audience made her a true film icon.

But she was much more than a movie star. Above all, Audrey Hepburn was an advocate for children, both personally and globally. At the height of her extraordinary career, she left Hollywood to concentrate on raising her children, a decision virtually unheard of among successful actresses. And then as UNICEF ambassador, she devoted the last part of her life, until her death, to bringing aid and comfort to children in the most ravaged places in the world.

Audrey Hepburn once said, "…it all starts with kindness. What a different world this could be if everyone lived by that."

–Leslie Koresky

CPSIA information can be obtained at www.ICGtesting.com
Printed in the USA
LVOW07s1019091016

508017LV00001B/24/P